Natalie

The Story of an Immigrant

BEATRIZ CURRY

iUniverse, Inc.
Bloomington

Natalie
The Story of an Immigrant

iUniverse books may be ordered through booksellers or by contacting:

iUniverse
1663 Liberty Drive
Bloomington, IN 47403
www.iuniverse.com
1-800-Authors (1-800-288-4677)

ISBN: 978-1-4759-1172-5 (sc)
ISBN: 978-1-4759-1174-9 (hc)
ISBN: 978-1-4759-1173-2 (ebk)

Printed in the United States of America

iUniverse rev. date: 04/26/2012

CONTENTS

ACKNOWLEDGMENTS

I WANT TO THANK MY husband David Curry with all my heart for helping me with his love, encouragement and the translation of this book. Thanks you for believing in me.

THANKS TO MY THREE DAUGHTERS, Beatriz, Patricia and Victoria for all their love, suggestions and for being by my side.

THANKS TO MY SON ALFONSO who gave me so much happiness and taught me so many things in English.

MANY THANKS TO MY SON Miguel for his patience and help in editing and correcting this book.

CHAPTER 1

A RAT THE SIZE OF A RABBIT

NATALIE DE LA CRUZ ARRIVED at the graduation ceremony of her youngest son elegantly dressed in blue, excited and transpiring in the muggy weather of South Florida in May. The main square of the University of Miami was crowded with happy families and jubilant students full of dreams and expectations. The Dean of the Architecture School addressed the audience, praising the newly graduates' achievements, and exalting the brilliant future awaiting them in this nation of opportunities. The entire square exploded in applauses. Then, one by one, the proud students walked across the stage to receive their hard-won diplomas. When Natalie heard her son's name, she was overcome by emotion and her eyes blurred with tears.

Her mind flashed back to that frightful day, 17 years earlier, and saw the stone-cold face of the immigration officer who emptied her purse on the desk, looking for reasons to send her back to her country of origin. He tried to remove her photo from the passport, arguing it was faked. He demanded to see how much money she had brought to the United States to pay for her vacation. She handed him a neatly rolled wad of dollar bills. He suspiciously counted to the last dollar: $3050. In reality, Natalie was not on vacation and she only had 1,300 dollars to tackle her new life in the United States with four children in tow.

Natalie also remembered the distant day she found her 12-year-old daughter in tears, sweltering, her face red-hot, in the corner of the filthy restaurant kitchen where she was working for $10 washing dishes every Sunday. Natalie also recalled the plastic-bag factory she worked at for three long years among deafening machines that numbed the soul and mind of the operators. But she fought back by writing poems among moving metals and turning pulleys. Ironically, in this same hellish factory she found the real treasures of life, which changed her destiny and that of her children in ways she would never have imagined. Almost two decades later, She was witnessing one of her most important triumph: the graduation of her youngest son, Adrian, as an architect. "It was all worth it," she mumbled to herself, drying her cheeks with her handkerchief.

Natalie's life in the United States began in 1977 after she decided to leave her native Colombia. She arrived to the cosmopolitan city of Miami with her four children and many illusions in her sentimental mind. That year winter had arrived in Miami suddenly and unusually cold, taking her by surprise. Normally, the cool air that comes from the north starts in December, but this year it swept through Miami in early November, sending temperatures tumbling down into the low 40's. People took out their sweaters and old coats with the smell of mothballs, and Miami's downtown seemed like a small New York City. Natalie didn't expect Miami to be this cold. She came from a tropical city where nobody talked about weather because it changed little throughout the year; it was always hot, especially from May to November. Only from December to April was the city pleasantly cooled by the trade winds blowing across the Caribbean.

On one of those cold mornings in Miami, Natalie was looking out at the street through the window of the restaurant where she was working at. The restaurant opened at six o'clock and by then everything had to be ready for the customers, mostly retired low-income Americans who lived downtown in small rooms with no kitchens. They woke up early in the morning to take advantage of the cheap breakfast and coffee offered at the restaurant, making a line in front of the restaurant before it opened. The restaurant did not only offer them a hearty $1.99 breakfast, but also a place to escape to from inclement weather and other adversities on the street. It was also a good alternative to the limited menu and boring food offered by fast-food restaurants. Natalie smiled a little when she saw the old people lined up, wearing their funny old coats and woolen hats, which they probably had not used since they came from their cold regions to take refuge in the warm climate of South Florida.

Jose, the owner, opened the door punctually as he always did. He was a Cuban man who had been living in the United States since the Communist revolution took control over the island. He was a hard-working man whose whole life revolved around keeping his restaurant going. He was proud that the customers liked his food and service. He was forty-five years old, well groomed, quite and calm. He seldom lost his temper, not even when homeless people would slip into the restaurant to ask for handouts, bothering the customers with their filthy appearance and unpleasant odor. When this happened, Jose would confront them firmly but fairly, and would kindly ask them to leave, not without giving them some food.

This day the costumers came in faster than usual, being chased in by the cold weather outside. Normally, they would enter slower and with serious faces. They probably thought that if they showed much interest in the food, the owner would take advantage of this to raise prices. But that morning was different. They streamed in faster to occupy the ten tables in the dinning room and warm up. Then Jose told Natalie to start filling up the cups with coffee. The restaurant was small but very clean and organized. The heater was on and the temperature was comfortable. In minutes the restaurant was full, and Natalie and the other waitress, Nohemi, served the coffee. Later, the two women started taking the orders. Nohemi was faster and more efficient than Natalie since she had more experience and liked her job. Natalie had difficulties understanding old people ordering their food. They often woke up in a bad mood and refused to repeat themselves. She had studied English in her Spanish-speaking country before arriving in the United States, but it is one thing to speak and read in school and quite another to understand grumpy old men ordering food at a restaurant in the U.S. Perhaps American customers asked themselves why would a foreign woman who didn't understand their language properly was working there instead of one of their own. But they seldom complained; if they did, Jose would answer that it was very difficult to hire American waitresses to work in Downtown Miami for the wages he could afford to pay. Besides, this was a commercial district ridden by crime and homelessness. During the day, executives and tourists filled the streets at a frantic pace. But when night fell, a different kind of humanity took over the street: homeless people and obscure figures lurked in the dark, like ghosts, looking for the residues abandoned by an affluent society. For this reason, customers accepted the immigrant waitress who confused over-easy with well-done eggs at a restaurant that charged little for the amount and quality of food served.

Jose's wife, Irma, a very active young woman, gave Natalie a list of the tables she needed to wait on. She told her to pay more attention when they talked and look at the customer's mouth very closely, which for Natalie meant being exposed to the bad breath of her morning costumers. She knew many of them did not shower in the morning, and some did not even brush their teeth. Finally, Natalie took three orders, while Nohemi finished the rest. Natalie frequently forgot things in the kitchen, and had to work more. This irritated Maria, the cook, who was quick to humiliate her.

"You are always forgetting something; I don't know how Jose puts up with you. If it were up to me, you would be out on the street,"

Maria complained offensively.

Natalie didn't answer. She needed the job and knew that the cook was the most important person in the restaurant. Maria was sixty years old, small, blond and irritable. Despite her biter disposition, she worked fast and effectively, like a young woman. She was very proud of her Mediterranean origin and her ability to cook good food. Natalie knew that she had to put up with her and didn't pay much attention to her inflammatory remarks.

At three o'clock Natalie and Nohemi's shift ended. Then they ate their lunch and distributed their tips, which was not much. Most customers would only leave 25-cent tips. That day, Natalie received ten dollars, enough to buy a couple of coats for her children at the flea market, she thought. Before they left, the two women had to clean the place, sweep and mop the floor, and leave everything ready for the night shift. Mopping the floor was very hard for Natalie, her hands were weak, and she was not used to it. She wore gloves, but the filthy, stinking water made her nauseous. The floor was too wet and Jose told her:

"You don't have the strength to do anything. It would be better if you eat steak."

"But you don't give us steak to eat." She answered jokingly.

"Because steaks are expensive, but you can buy one if you want."

Natalie wanted to tell him that she wasn't accustomed to doing this; that she had maids in her country, that her house was big, that she never had to cook, and that she never had to pick up stubs. But she stayed quiet. He wouldn't believe her anyway, and he would probably answer:

"Everybody says the same thing. If you were like a queen in your country, why are you here?"

"Mop again, Natalie," Jose insisted, "I don't want somebody to fall because of you. Then I would have to pay their medical bills. Do you understand that?"

"Yes, don't worry, I will mop again."

She went to the kitchen, bucket and the mop in hands to ask Luis, the dishwasher, to help her wring out the mop. She offered him one dollar. He did it, looked at her and smiled:

"You look like a delicate woman, how old are you?" He asked.

"Thirty four, she answered. Why do you ask?"

"I am twenty four years old, but I like older woman. Young girls only think about makeup and buying clothes."

Natalie observed him. He was young, strong, ugly, ill mannered, and apparently proud of his bad manners and sloppy appearance.

"Thanks Luis," she said, "I have to clean the floor again."

"Tomorrow, I will do the floor for you. You know, I like you."

She didn't pay attention to his words and gave him the dollar. She mopped again and this time Jose was pleased.

Natalie felt very sad inside. She understood that kind of life was not for her. Nohemi was ready to go home; her husband was waiting for her holding a little girl in his arms. She seemed happy with her life. Natalie, on the other hand, was tormented by something inside she couldn't express. She took off her apron, combed her light-brown hair and put red lipstick on. But her dress was so impregnated with the smell of food that she couldn't bear herself. She wanted to arrive home soon to change her clothes and take a bath. Suddenly, she smiled, showing her white teeth and her big sweet smile. She would see her children soon. She would pick them up at their school located only a block away from the restaurant. It was a good school named Gesu Parish School. They were already speaking some English and getting adjusted to their new life. Her children were her only happiness in the United States.

When she walked outside, a gust of cold air pierced through her entire body.

"I am going to have to buy coats for the children," she thought.

"The light sweaters they have are not enough. They could catch a bad cold. They don't have insurance, and doctors in this country are very expensive."

She was about to cry when she arrived at the school. Her children waited for her at four o'clock every day. Soon she was in front of the fence that separated the school from the street. She looked around trying to find them among the large groups of students leaving the school. She spotted them and all her worries dissipated; she was all smiles. She had two girls and one boy at this school. The oldest girl, Eugenia, was attending another school. Rosa was twelve years old, had long blond hair, a pretty face and amber eyes. Maria was ten years old, with long black hair and a beautiful face with dark eyes. The boy, Adrian, was seven years old, a little skinny and a bit tall for his age. Darker than his sisters, he was of an exotic beauty with big inquisitive eyes. Being the youngest one, he was very close to his mother. He was the first that ran to the gate to meet Natalie, hugging her with love. Natalie kissed all three very affectionately. The girls wore uniforms, blue scarves and white blouses. Adrian wore dark-blue pants and a white shirt.

Gesu was probably the only school in Downtown Miami and certainly the only one to accept foreign students without asking too many questions. Natalie believed she was lucky to have found this school so close to the restaurant. Her children were happy there, especially with their English teacher who went out of his way to teach them the new language. She paid fifty dollars a month for the three children, which was not bad for a Catholic school.

Natalie and her children were walking very content along the sidewalk, looking at the stores and all the pretty things on display, even though they couldn't buy anything. Only Adrian insisted on buying a toy car with batteries that he saw on a display in one of the stores.

"It will have to be on Saturday when Jose pays me my week's salary. Now I don't have enough money, we have to buy coats." Natalie responded.

"But I want it today." He insisted.

"Adrian, it's not possible today; didn't you hear what mother said?" Rosa told him in a very serious voice.

"We have to buy the coats for the cold weather." Maria added.

"I know it's too cold, but I have to go to the bank first, and take money from my savings account." Natalie answered.

Natalie's apartment was on the second floor of an old five-story building. She chose the second floor because there was no elevator. The place wasn't exactly an apartment; it was a studio, but it fit her budget and was close to her job. Studio was a fancy word for a small room with a miniature kitchen and a bathroom. The furniture consisted of a queen bed, sofa, and small dining table with four chairs. The tiny kitchen had a refrigerator and an electric stove. A bathroom and a closet completed the dwelling. Natalie divided the room with a nice curtain so that the bed couldn't be seen from the door; only the small "living room" was visible. She bought a television, some plants and pictures to change the look of the decrepit studio into something more lively, perhaps reflecting her tropical background. The girls loved it.

That afternoon Natalie bought the coats for her and her children, and surprised Adrian with the battery-powered car he wanted so much. The girls looked very pretty in their navy-blue coats and berets she bought for the cold weather. Rosa looked at herself in the mirror and smiled.

"Don't you like it? Maria asked her.

"Yes, but it is a bit large."

"That's better," Natalie said. "This way you won't feel the cold so much. They said this year the winter would be very harsh."

Adrian didn't care about the coat; he took the toy car off the package immediately and started to play. He put the car on the floor and it sped off towards the kitchen. The boy ran behind the little toy and suddenly he screamed in terror. They all panicked and ran to the kitchen. He was in the corner of the kitchen with the toy in his hand, his face very pale, looking toward the stove.

A huge rat jumped from the stove to the floor and ran around the room creating total chaos in the small apartment. The girls screamed and climbed on the bed. Natalie carried Adrian and they jumped on the bed too. They were all scared, the children hugging their mother until the rat disappeared. Natalie tried to calm them down.

"Don't worry dears, the rat is gone."

"No mami, the rat can't leave, it is locked in here." Rosa said.

"No, I'm sure they have a hole that we cannot see, but I will go talk with the manager anyway. He has to change the apartment for us today." Natalie said.

"If they don't want to move us, what will we do? I won't sleep here with this big rat." Maria said.

"Me either," said Rosa. "I will go to sleep in Margarita's apartment."

Natalie tried to persuade them,

"No we don't go to the neighbor's apartment; we are going to see the manager right now. He has to change us to another apartment. This is not allowed in this country, it's against the law."

Natalie's voice was firm, and the children noticed that their mother was very upset.

The manager's apartment was on the first floor. The manager was surprised and notably upset when he saw Natalie with her four children. He and his wife were older people who shared a disdain for Natalie's family. Whether they didn't like children or hated the fact that her family was living cramped in a small studio, Natalie was not sure. The reason they were accepted in the building in the first place was because Irma put a good word for them.

"Didn't you see the notice on the door? It says that we were only open until six o'clock and it is almost seven." The man said rudely.

"I know," Natalie answered, "but it is very important because we can not sleep in that apartment tonight, that is why we are here."

"Why not?"

The man asked very surprised, and the woman stopped eating her rice with chicken to listen to Natalie.

"Because there is a rat in my apartment the size of a rabbit. My children are terrified. We are here because we want another apartment."

"Did you say a rat?" The manager questioned. "No, I don't believe that. There are no rats in my building."

"But, I swear we saw one that terrified all of us."

"We don't have another apartment available."

The woman said, while she wolfed down the chicken.

"I am sorry, but you will have to look for one."

Natalie's voice was calm but firm. She and her children sat down on their sofa. They were a little scared thinking that the managers wouldn't change them to another apartment.

The managers ignored then for a while, and continued devouring the last bones on their plates. Natalie and her children were silent waiting for an answer. She felt kind of nervous, but she didn't show it. She knew that they had a bigger apartment on the third floor available. The woman looked at her and finally asked:

"What do you think you are doing? You are not staying here all night."

"We don't have any other option; we can't stay in a place where there are rats. They can bite my children. Then, what are you going to do? This is a very serious problem."

Natalie looked at her without fear. She was fighting for her children and she would not back down. The couple was silent and looked at each other when they heard Natalie's words regarding the danger posed to her children. Finally the manager asked Natalie:

"Would you pay twenty dollars more? The apartments on the third floor are more expensive."

Natalie was mentally figuring out her income. She could pay it, although she would be very short for other things, but this was an emergency and she answered determinedly,

"Okay, I will pay it, but I don't think it's fair."

"Well, do you want it or not?"

"I already told you, yes."

"Then, take the key. Will you pay me tomorrow?"

"I can't tomorrow; I will pay you on Saturday when Irma pays me."

The man gave the key to Natalie, and she left the manager's apartment followed by her children who went running up the stairs eager to see the new apartment that would hopefully have no rats. That night they moved to the other apartment, transferring their few possessions, including their most precious one: a black-and-white television set, which cost them one hundred dollar. The three girls moved their clothes to the new closet and helped Natalie put away the kitchen utensils and the rest of their things. Adrian with his new toy asked his mother if he could play with it again.

"Yes you can, but you know it's time to go to bed very soon."

"We haven't eaten mami," Maria said, "I am hungry."

Natalie smiled; she was right, she had forgotten to cook for them with all the commotion of the evening.

"Don't worry dears, I am going to make some sandwiches."

Natalie had scored a small victory in her hard life as an immigrant.

CHAPTER 2

1,300 DOLLARS AND A DREAM

NATALIE HAD ARRIVED IN MIAMI three months earlier. Back in her native Colombia, she had lived through a long troublesome marriage that ended in separation. Natalie decided that leaving the country was her only option. She was fed up with the closed mindedness and backwardness of the people in her hometown. They were quick to judge, criticize, and even destroy those who did not adhere to their conventions. They rejected modernity and condemned a woman to be a slave in a marriage where she couldn't find happiness. She couldn't endure this situation any longer so she sold the small hotel by the beach she owned, paid her bills, and bought the airplane tickets to Miami.

On a rainy September day Natalie De La Cruz abandoned her country with her four children. She left behind her mother, sisters, brother, family, friends, work, and everything she loved and knew. It was a very sad day, but she couldn't go on living the way she had been. She had to change her life, to start afresh in a new country. She wanted to be happy with her children, to offer them a better future, an education in a more open society. She wished to be free at last from the restraining force of her traditional society, from the imprisonment she felt in her hometown. For this reason she shut the past, erased her memories, threw way old pictures and looked towards the future. The future was the only thing for her and her children, but she knew this was not going to be easy.

Ever since she first set foot on the Miami International Airport, she felt a strong force against potential immigrants. After they arrived, Natalie and her four children quickly forgot the sadness of leaving their country and became exited and happy to see the big airport and all the new things they had never seen before. She was wearing a pretty blue dress and her slender body looked very attractive. She had light-brown hair down to her shoulders and her gracious face looked happy. The three girls, Eugenia, Rosa and Maria looked like dolls, wearing cute dresses and well combed hair. Adrian was too young to understand what was going on, his big eyes observing everything around him, possibly wondering why he was there.

They waited in line for immigration for a long time. The three girls were a little bored and Adrian started to play with his toy car on the carpet. Finally, it was their turn before the immigration officer—one of the most critical moments in the immigrants' tortuous journey. It was an American woman and she looked at Natalie very seriously, asking her some questions in English. Natalie understood and answered correctly: they were on vacation and wanted to stay for a month to take the children to Disney World and maybe take a trip to Boston.

"Do you have family in Boston?" She asked.

"No," Natalie answered.

Natalie had a relative in Boston, but somebody had told her not to mention any family in the U.S. That could raise suspicion that she may be planning to stay in this country. But mentioning Boston was probably not a good idea. That was a mistake, but she realized it too late. The woman didn't stamp their passport.

"You have to wait one moment. Please go to that office," Natalie was told.

"Which office?" Natalie asked a little nervous."

"Strait ahead," she said "and hurry up there are people waiting."

Then Natalie grabbed her children and went to the place the woman indicated.

She didn't know what was going on; her passport and American visa were correct; she didn't understand why she was singled out. She opened the door and they entered the office. Nobody was there; she and the children sat on a sofa, waiting for somebody to appear. The girls asked her what had happened and she tried to be calm:

"Nothing happened, something about immigration, but soon we will be out of here."

Half an hour later and they were still waiting. By now Natalie had become increasingly nervous; she stood up to leave when a man walked in. He was a young American man, tall and good looking, but with a dark frown on his face. Natalie took that as a bad sign. He looked at her and didn't say hello, he only said with a cold voice in perfect Spanish: "Come to my desk, and leave the children over there."

The children looked at the man in disbelieve and stayed in the same place. Adrian tried to follow his mother, but Rosa grabbed him by his hand and told him to sit down.

Natalie sat in front of the man. He had her passport in his hand. She felt nervous, faked a smile and asked if she could have a cigarette from the pack she saw on his desk. It was the time when smoking was very common and allowed everywhere. So it was not impolite to ask for a cigarette. However, the look in the man's eyes, blue and strong, made her feel insignificant and stupid. He didn't answer and Natalie thought this man had the coldest and most hostile eyes she had ever seen. She didn't smile anymore and waited for him to say something.

"Are you Natalie De La Cruz, and are these your children?"

He asked her, looking at Natalie's picture on the passport.

"Yes," she said.

"How much money did you bring to support them here for a month to go to Disney World and Boston?"

"I brought what is necessary."

"Give me your purse."

"Why?"

"I need to see it."

When he said that, his tone of voice was high and rude.

She gave it to him immediately, surprised because she thought he didn't have the right to do that.

"Please, don't raise your voice," she said. "You will scare my children."

The man looked at her, but he didn't answer. He opened Natalie's purse and emptied everything, including her personal items, and spread them on the desk. She was shocked to see all her personal papers, gas receipts, airplane tickets, identification cards, etc, displayed on his desk. After he examined each item, he started to look for the money, and he found it in the double lining of her purse. He counted the wad of cash, dollar bill by dollar bill, totaling $3050. In reality she only owned $1300, the rest belonged to a friend back in Colombia who asked her to buy something to send back to Colombia. Finally he said,

"You can put everything back in your purse."

She did what she was told. She felt humiliated for his rudeness. Natalie was looking at him, waiting to see what was next. She thought maybe he would send them back to their country, but to do that he had to have a reason. He proceeded, observing her passport and comparing the pictures on her passport with her face. Then, he checked the pictures of her children and looked at them. He closed the passport and asked her:

"How long do you want to be in the United States?"

"The amount of time you want to give us."

"If it was up to me, not one day. I don't think this is even your picture," He continued.

Natalie lost her patience, stood up and confronted him.

"Listen Mr. Immigration, because you don't give your name, in my country I worked at a travel agency. I know about tourism, if you think my passport is faked go ahead and take my fingerprints. When Americans go to my country and loose something like their passport, they go to my office for help. You know what I do? Are you listening? I go with them to the bank to give them their new travelers checks with my signature because they don't have a passport or any other form of identification. Then I call the American Embassy in Bogotá to get new passports for them. We help them with everything. We don't threat them like you did to us, very rude and impolite."

Natalie was so mad that at this point she didn't care if the man would send them back to her country. She stood in front of him, looking into his eyes, without hesitation. Then the man changed his attitude and looked at her with certain surprise and admiration.

"I am sorry," he said, "but I had to be sure that you had enough money to support your children in this country. I am going to give you one month to stay here, if you want more time you have to go to the Immigration Office for an extension."

He stamped the passport and gave it back to her. Natalie didn't say a word and left the room with her children. Her heart was beating very rapidly but she felt proud of herself. It was her first problem in this new country and was the beginning of a large chain of troubles she never imagined. But for now she smiled again oblivious to what she was getting into. They took a taxi to the hotel she had reserved.

The hotel was not fancy but clean and comfortable. It was located in Miami Beach, very close to the ocean. The children were very happy the first day in Miami, and went out with their mother to see many new things they had never seen before. Later, they went to the beach, played with the waves and stayed there all afternoon. At night they ate at a restaurant hamburgers and hot dogs. Natalie spent more money than she had planned the first day, but the children needed to have a good time, later she would look for another place cheaper where they could live.

The following week Natalie tried to find a small apartment on the beach, but she always got the same absurd answer: "No children, no pets." To reject children was to repudiate the very essence of humanity, she thought disconcerted. In her native country that was unheard of. But Miami Beach was a city of old people, a magnet for retirees from all over the United Sates looking for warmer climate and affordable apartments close to the beach. In fact, the now famous and clamorous South Beach was nothing but a depressing run-down district crowded with old people, sitting in front of Art-Deco era buildings.

"I have to find something where we can live, not a hotel but an apartment we can afford."

Natalie told her children. But most managers of the apartment buildings didn't answer, and if they did, they shut the door on her face. She had no choice but to pay another week at the hotel. She started to look for a job in the travel agencies around the neighborhood, leaving the responsibility of the children to Rosa who was a very responsible girl. She filled out many applications, but she couldn't find anything. She had experience, but her experience and references were from another country, and her English was far from perfect. To make matters worse, computers were starting to replace the books that Natalie was used to her country. She would have to take a computer course and learn the new system to get a job. That means studying more English, which was impossible if she was to support her four children. She understood that was out of the question for now.

After looking for a job all day, she came back to the hotel disenchanted. That night she cried in the bed when her children were sleeping, and she made the decision to find another kind of job.

"Tomorrow I will go to another place. I have to be strong and I will find a job no matter what, even if something I am not accustomed to."

The next day, Natalie and her children took the bus to Downtown Miami. She told the children they were going to have breakfast at McDonalds. They liked to eat there, which was like a party. Natalie ordered breakfast for them. But she could only drink a cup of coffee. She had seen at nearby cafeteria a sign that said: "Waitress wanted." She didn't know anything about this job but she would learn, Natalie thought. She was desperate, everyday her lifeline got thinner. They simply could not spend more money. She told Eugenia to stay with the rest of the children.

"I want to go in there to apply for a job."

"But mami, you don't know anything about working at a restaurant."

"I know, but I have to try, we cannot keep going like this. Very soon we won't have anything."

She was talking to Rosa and Eugenia discretely, trying not to let Maria and Adrian know what she was doing. She didn't think they would understand.

"I will come back in a few minutes." She said. "Where are you going mami?"

The two children asked.

"Don't worry, it's across the street, I am going to see what they have on sale."

Natalie crossed the street and walked into the restaurant. It was small but very clean and pleasant. A young and attractive woman was taking care of some customers. She looked at Natalie and invited her to sit at a table.

"I am looking for a job." Natalie said. "I would like to talk to the manager please."

"He is not here now but I can help you."

"Oh, thank you, I saw the sign outside and I think I can do this job."

The woman looked at her and noticed that Natalie was pretty and well dressed.

"Do you have experience as a waitress?"

"No, but I know a lot about dealing with customers. I think I can learn quickly."

"That's good, we need a waitress that can work in the morning until three o'clock. Do you think you can do it?"

"Of course I can do it."

The woman's name was Irma and she told Natalie that she could start working the next day. Natalie was taken by surprise. Instead of the usual long application process that always ended up in rejection, she was offered a job on the spot. She couldn't believe it. But she felt it was too soon.

What about the children? She understood that she had to make a decision. Irma looked at her again; she noticed that she was hesitant.

"Not tomorrow," she said, "because I have three children and I have to get a school for them."

"Oh, that's not a problem, there is a very good school close to this restaurant. It is called Gesu School. When you finish your shift at three o'clock, you can pick them up."

Natalie looked at her and smiled, finally things seem to be working out for her.

"Oh thanks for telling me that. I am going right now to see the school."

"Where are your children?" Irma asked,

"They are across the street eating at MacDonald's, waiting for me."

"Then, are you coming tomorrow in the morning?"

"Well I have to talk with the people at the school."

"Okay, but you have to tell me today what you decide."

"Yes, I will come back in one hour probably."

That day was like a miracle for Natalie because she found a job and a school for her children.

After Natalie started working, Irma helped her get the studio close to the restaurant, and Natalie began the long and painful process of adaptation to a new society, a new country and a new world. After one month, Natalie learned the ropes and became a waitress. She took care of the customers faster and more efficiently, understood their orders and memorized their likings. Most customers ordered the same every time. She even befriended them, and some would give her good tips.

Her relationship with Maria, the cook, improved a bit. Natalie worked very hard, going beyond her waitress duties, cleaning and washing the glasses and cups they needed regularly. She tried to do everything right to please Maria, hoping to get along better. However, this period of relative peace between them came to an end one morning.

At eleven o'clock Jose wrote on the blackboard the specials of the day. It was placed on a visible spot where costumers could see it. Five orders were on the daily specials that day. Jose numbered each one so it was easy for Natalie to write down and order in the kitchen. A family of Latin American tourists came that day for lunch. There were five people, the parents and three children. Natalie took care of them cordially. She brought water and bread and pointed towards the blackboard with the specials for the day. They chose number three: palomilla steak, rice and beans. This was a very popular dish among Latin Americans, the price was good and the food was delicious. It was like homemade food for them. Natalie took her pad, wrote the orders, and later brought the sodas they had ordered.

The family was nice and asked Natalie about Disney World and other places of entertainment for the children. Natalie told them about Disney World and everything she knew about the park since she had been there before. While talking to them she made a mistake and wrote 5 instead of 3, which meant "chicken and pork fried rice," the most hated dish by Maria because it took a lot of work and preparations to make.

Natalie didn't notice the mistake until Maria rang the little bell announcing the food was ready for the costumers. Then Natalie looked at the plates and felt her heart palpitating faster. "It is the end," she thought, the order was a mistake and there were five orders. She didn't say anything, took the plates, and put them on the costumer's table. They looked at the food, and noticed that it was very different from what they had ordered." Where are the steaks?" The father asked.

"Well it's fried rice with chicken and pork, that's what you ordered, it's very good." Natalie answered in a soft voice with the hope Maria didn't find out about her mistake, but they kept looking at the food inquisitively.

"We ordered the number three." The woman said clearly.

"Oh, I am sorry I made a mistake, I wrote down the wrong number. Forgive me, please."

The family didn't answer anything just looked at Natalie's sad face, but Nohemi found out what happened and told Maria about Natalie's mistake. Maria came out of the kitchen with her dirty apron, her hair full of grease and sweat. Jose and Irma weren't there at that time, and Maria considered herself the owner of the restaurant. The tourist family was looking at the food in front of them and probably would have started to eat, but Maria's loud voice paralyzed them.

"Take back the plates, Nohemi," she said, "I am going to cook what they wanted. "What did they order Natalie?"

"Number three." She said.

"How can you make that kind of mistake? I am going to talk to Jose about this problem. All you want is to drive this restaurant out of business with that kind of service. I won't allow this."

She returned to the kitchen to start cooking the food they originally ordered. Maria was furious, she made a lot of noise with the plates and pans, it was so loud in the kitchen that the family began to be concerned. They were moving their heads in disapproval. Natalie was silent; she didn't move to pick up the plates that were on the table. Nohemi tried, but the father told her they didn't have time to wait and that they will eat the chicken and pork fried rice.

"Tell the cook not to prepare anything. We are good with this."

Nohemi moved rapidly to stop Maria from cooking the other food. Then Natalie went back to them, and said,

"Thanks, you are very nice, please come back and I will promise it will not happen again. You know it is my first job in this country and sometimes I make mistakes."

She smiled and the family smiled back. One of the children said:

"This rice is delicious."

"Yes," the mother said, "and that woman in the kitchen is terrible, I guess you don't have a good time here."

"No, but for now I have to stay here."

Natalie appreciated the strangers' comments; they recognized how unfair Maria was to Natalie. The family left and told Natalie they would come back. She felt a little better, but she knew that incident wouldn't stop there. And sure enough, Maria told Jose about Natalie's mistake, and he talked to Irma. She was very serious,

"Please, pay more attention to what you are doing. You know Jose, he is very disappointed on you and next time you will not be allowed to continue working at the restaurant."

Listening to Irma's words made Natalie very sad. She thought it would be better to look for another job than continuing at war with Maria. She knew Maria wouldn't stop until she left the restaurant for good.

CHAPTER 3

MIAMI BEACH

NATALIE WAS OFF THE NEXT day. She was reading the newspaper and found and ad in the employment section asking for a waitress with experience in Miami Beach. After her children left for school, she decided to go to Miami Beach to give it a try.

"I have some experience, no matter what Maria says about me."

Around ten o'clock in the morning Natalie took a bus to Miami Beach. During the trip she enjoyed the view of Biscayne Bay on both sides of causeway, the high-rise buildings and the elegant hotels that bordered the beach. She felt relaxed and a little happy because the ocean view always produced peace within her. She got off the bus at the Lincoln Road Mall.

This was a very popular spot with tourists enjoying the many stores, restaurants and cafés. The place Natalie was looking for was nearby and she walked on the sidewalk at brisk pace, her high heels resonating rhythmically. This attracted the attention of some men who were passing by. They were not tourists but immigrants like her. One of them told her in Spanish:

"You have very pretty legs".

She didn't look at him and kept walking.

She passed by the Livingston Hotel and smiled, remembering the two times she had stayed there when she was working for the travel agency in her country. It was a sumptuous hotel with large salons decorated in gold color that dazzled her the first time she visited. She stayed there for one week as part of a large travel agency convention to promote tourism between the US and Latin America. She had a marvelous week with the group, visiting places, shopping and eating at elegant restaurants. That was part of her happy past. Now everything was different; she wasn't a tourist or a proud delegate anymore, but an immigrant woman looking for a job to survive with four children—a big responsibility on her shoulders.

The man who had said something to her a few minutes earlier was walking behind her. She looked at him when he was close. He was a Latin man in his mid thirties. He asked Natalie:

"Do you need company? I can show you Miami Beach, you look like a tourist."

"Leave me alone please."

She answered a little angry, and the man got the message. He stopped and waited maybe for a more accessible woman.

Natalie continued looking for the address of the restaurant. She then saw a car leaving a hotel and the driver stared at her. He beeped at her softly and made a gesture inviting her into his car. This made her feel bad and chose to ignore him. She thought that her green dress was too sexy or simply that men in this city were disrespectful towards women.

Finally, she found the address and walked in with determination. She knew that a positive attitude would help her to get the job. The place was a store for tourists, selling everything from magazines to sunglasses, postcards and all kinds of souvenirs. It was a gift shop for your typical tourist. In the back of the store there was a cafeteria with several tables covered with white tablecloths. They sold hot dogs, hamburgers, salads, ice creams, snacks and a few other things.

The man in charge was busy at that moment preparing hamburgers for customers. She liked the place and looked with interest at the people who were waiting. They were older people possibly in their sixties; the majority of them women, clothed in colorful dresses and wearing sun hats. They were speaking English without an accent, which Natalie was able to understand. She sat down at the counter and observed the man who was working alone; he was fast, taking orders and cooking on the grill. He also took care of the register and still had time to joke around with the costumers. He spoke English well but with a Latin accent. He looked like he was in his mid-thirties. He had an attractive presence and joyful personality. When he finished with his costumers, he looked at Natalie and asked her what she would like.

"I want a coffee, please" She spoke in English, but he answered in Spanish.

"One coffee only? Wouldn't you like something to eat?"

"No, thank you; maybe later."

The man's clear eyes, looked at Natalie with attention and a glimmer of admiration, but Natalie didn't notice it. She was too busy thinking how to ask about the job. His name was René; she knew that because an American lady called him to order ice cream. He served the ice cream in a cone, but it was crooked and it looked like it was going to fall off. The lady, in her late sixties and probably retired, moved back a little, fearful of getting a stain on her dress, but René straightened it with a quick reaction and he gave it to her perfectly. She smiled happily; she liked his game, maybe she found some distraction from her daily routine in this beautiful place called Miami Beach. Natalie thought at that moment that ageing for Americans was a sad affair. They chose to retire away from their families, especially children, came to a warmer place like Miami and led lonely lives. That was something Natalie couldn't understand, but maybe they wanted a better climate or they preferred being alone or they had a family that didn't appreciate them or they liked their independence. Her thoughts were interrupted when René brought her coffee and cream and put it in front of her with courtesy. Then he brought a glass of water. She smiled and said, "thank you."

He leaned over the counter and asked:

"I have never seen you around here before. Are you a tourist"?

"No, I am not a tourist." She said.

Natalie took a sip of American coffee and thought that this would be the right moment to ask about the job. She asked the man about the job that was advertised on the newspaper. Then he said:

"are you applying for the waitress job?"

"Yes, I read your advertisement on the newspaper for a waitress."

He was a little surprised.

"Are you looking for a job?"

"Yes, that is the reason I am here."

"Well; I am going to give you an application to fill out. The owner is not here now, but he will come back in the afternoon after two o'clock. Please, excuse me for asking this question. Are you a resident of the United States?"

"Yes," she said with a firm voice. She wasn't of course, but couldn't tell him the truth. This seemed like a good place to work and she didn't want to miss the opportunity. René brought the application, and Natalie started filling it out. René went to wait on another costumer who ordered a hot dog. She listened to him talking and laughing with the old man. René seemed like a friendly guy.

Natalie spent ten minutes filling out the application. She then reviewed it carefully, got up and walked towards René. He took the application and looked at Natalie head to toe, his eyes lighted up observing her body. He stared almost insolently, sparing nothing, hair, dress, legs, black-leather shoes. Natalie didn't like it, and she felt uneasy and walked towards the door. He noticed and said:

"Please, don't go, you didn't tell me your name."

"My name is Natalie, it is on my application."

"I see, the manager will give you the job if you have some experience."

"Yes I have," she answered a little more calm. "I am working now at a restaurant in downtown Miami."

René made a gesture as though he didn't like it, and said:

"Downtown is not a good place for a pretty woman like you."

"Thanks, but I have never had any problems with people there, it's just that I want to work in Miami Beach."

"Then come back at two o'clock, and I will have an answer"

"Okay, thank you, I will come back at that time."

Natalie left, and René looked at her as she walked out of the restaurant, then he went back to his customers.

It was a pretty day with a pleasant breeze coming from the ocean and the sun was brilliant over Miami Beach. For some reason Natalie always felt happy there. She walked on the streets among tourists, enjoying the breeze and the beautiful day. She nodded smiling at some old ladies walking by. She walked into a store to buy something for her children. The store had a special sale for that day and she bought two dresses for Rosa and Maria, and a pair of jeans for Adrian. She didn't forget to buy a toy car for his collection. She spent twenty dollars, well over her budget, but she didn't care. It was a special day, and she was going to get a better job. At least that was her naïve mind was thinking.

She returned to the cafeteria at two o'clock as René asked her. The store was full and she had to wait half an hour until he finished serving the costumers. He was working very hard and she noticed that he needed help. Finally the restaurant was empty and she walked up to him and asked about the manager.

"Yes, he was here. But he didn't give me a hand with all the customers that I had to take care of. He said that he didn't feel good and left without any regards for me. He is an inconsiderate American."

René was angry, and Natalie understood that she came at a bad time. She didn't say anything. René didn't mention talking to the manger about her so she felt discouraged. Maybe they had offered the job to somebody else.

She told René:

"Thank you Anyway. If you still need somebody, call me on the phone. I put the number on the application."

She started to walk to the door with her packages and purse, but the man stopped her.

"Wait, I talked to the manager about you. I am sorry that I was a little upset, but I am alone here and it is to much work for one person."

"Yes, I understand."

He finished washing the dishes, cleaned his hands on the apron, came close to her and said,

"Listen Natalie, Mr. Anderson told me that I can hire you if I though you could do the job. I want to give you the opportunity. I think you could learn fast. It's not difficult, only the English, but if you understand some English there shouldn't be a problem."

She smiled.

"Then will you give me a job?"

"Yes, but I have to explain something. The shift starts at three o'clock and finishes at eleven or twelve depending on how many customers we have. He pays $70.00 a week plus tips."

She listened carefully and felt very disenchanted. This shift was impossible for her. She lived far and she didn't have transportation, she couldn't leave the children alone so late.

He noticed the change in her expression.

"What happened, do you have a problem?"

"Yes, the shift is very late for me. I have small children that will be waiting for me."

"How many children do you have?"

"I have four, and the oldest is only 14 years old."

"Do you have a husband?"

His question was direct and too indiscrete for Natalie. She didn't answer and thought it was not his business to inquire about her private life. She was waiting for him to continue, but he didn't. He understood that Natalie didn't like his questions. He was sure the young woman didn't have a husband as she turned very seriously when he asked.

"But we have to think of something if you want to work here?"

"Like what?" She said.

"You can take the bus at ten o'clock at night until you can get a car, or you can move closer to here. I know about some nice apartments you can walk to from here."

"Do you think this would be possible?"

"For sure, you can start to work today if you want to."

"Today is not possible, I don't have appropriate clothes, besides I have to talk with my friend, and ask her if she can stay with my children until I come back."

He looked at her and made a boring gesture with his mouth.

"I want to help you, but you have to try. You can use an apron and call your friend on this phone. In case you cannot take the bus I can take you when I finish."

"Thanks, but I don't think it's possible. I have to do many things before I make that decision."

René was clearly a man with a lot of experience, and he knew how to convince a woman.

"Listen Natalie, if you don't stay now you are going to loose the opportunity to work here. I will have to take someone else; I cannot do all these by myself. You can start selling the ice cream, which too much of my time. Besides, you can help me clean the tables, wash the dishes and other simple things. This is an easy job; I will take care of more complicated things. You don't have to cook or anything like that; that is my job. Don't you worry Natalie everything will be okay. This place is very relaxing, not like downtown. You can leave anytime and nobody is going to bother you."

Natalie listened, thought about Maria, the children, and immediately made up her mind.

"Deal."

CHAPTER 4

LEARNING THE HARD WAY

THAT AFTERNOON WENT BY FAST for Natalie. She served ice cream cones to customers, mostly older American ladies, colorfully dressed like young girls and wearing earrings and large necklaces. She liked them because they looked happier than the old men downtown. They also looked wealthier judging by the way they dressed and the bags they carried. Tips were meager, ten cents per customer was the rule, but by nightfall the glass of the tips was full. Natalie noticed that René put his tips in the same glass. She thought he would split the tips later, like she did with Nohemi. At seven o'clock René called her and told her to sit down and eat dinner. She wasn't hungry, but he insisted and cooked a hamburger with french-fries for her and served them with and a glass of milk.

"You have to eat," he said, "if not, you are going to be too skinny and you won't have any energy to work."

Natalie smiled and thanked him. She sat down, took off her uncomfortable high heel shoes and she felt better. She started to eat, but remembered her children being alone, which made her feel guilty. She had been talking to Margarita, her neighbor, and she promised to stay with them for a while until they went to sleep. But she knew her girls and Adrian, and how impatient they could become because of her absence. She ate with no appetite, but like René said, she needed to eat. The work was easy and René seemed like a good man who wanted to help her. She would make twenty dollars more every week and that could be used to buy a used car they needed so much. That night was slow; she cleaned the tables, washed the glasses and put everything in order for the next day. However, when she wanted to take the mop to clean the floor, René stopped her saying,

"That's my job, you can fill the cooler with the sodas and juices."

Natalie was immersed in her work when she looked outside and saw a deserted street. She suddenly realized it was late. She got scared and asked René what time it was.

"It is ten thirty, your bus passed by a long time ago."

"Oh god, what am I going to do now? Why didn't you remind me?"

"I was distracted like you, but don't worry I will take you home."

"Where is your car?"

He took some time to answer.

"Close to my apartment."

"Where do you live?" she asked nervously.

"Just two blocks from here."

She felt anguished. It was eleven at night and her children were alone. She tried to hurry up and asked him to count the tips.

"You can count the change in the register, but the tips are all yours, we don't have to divide it."

"No, it is yours too."

"No Natalie, it is your first day, and I want you take something for your children."

"No, it is not fair."

René didn't pay attention to her words, and went ahead cleaning the floor. At that moment the owner, Mr. Anderson, came into the store. He was a mature man, tall and robust. He said hello to Natalie and talked to René. He opened the register and started to take the receipts and count the money. While they were doing that, Natalie knew that it had to be twelve o'clock. She was sitting in the chair silently thinking about what to do next. She felt a bad sensation inside. It was useless to continue waiting for René, and she made the decision to take a taxi. She stood up, grabbed her purse and her packages and started walking out. René noticed that and told her,

"Wait Natalie, don't leave alone, we are already finished."

"No René, I have to go, it's very late."

"But Natalie, what happened to you. I told you I would take you."

The two men closed the register, and proceeded to close the store. Finally the store was closed. The manager left in his fancy car that was parked nearby. Natalie thought with sadness that she would not be able come back the next day, it was impossible for her. They walked through the lonely street towards René's car in silent. Rene seemed a little serious and Natalie thought he was probably tired. They walked west away from the ocean for more than two blocks beyond Lincoln Road and the nice hotels. They came upon a depressed neighborhood of old decrepit apartment buildings and cheap hotels. Natalie was surprised to find such a rundown district so close to Lincoln Road. She though it was probably the oldest area in Miami Beach where tourists never went. René was walking fast and she was having a hard time keeping up with him. She was getting worried and impatient and asked him:

"Why do you park your car so far?"

He stopped for a moment to wait for her.

"I park my car where ever I can. Do you think it's too far?"

"Oh yes!"

"We have arrived already,"

He pointed towards an ugly looking building and led her into the lobby. It was an old rundown building several stories high, similar to the others in the neighborhood but with more broken windows. The "hotel" was neglected, the carpeting in the lobby dirty and stinking, the furniture old and broken.

Natalie didn't like the place; it looked poor and abandoned.

"Why did we come here?" She asked.

He looked at her a little disappointed.

"But Natalie, everything bothers you. I came here because it's my home, and I have to change my clothes because they smell like food."

"But it's late."

"I know, but I told you that I had to go to my apartment to change."

"Okay, I will wait for you here, but please come back fast."

"No Natalie, you can go up. There is a sitting room, besides you can see my apartment, and if you like it you can rent one here."

She looked at him and hesitated, not knowing what to do. Rene's face was serious, and he seemed like a good person trying to help her. She wanted to trust him. She followed him up the stairs to the third floor, but she had already decided not to move there. It was worse than her apartment downtown. When they arrived to third floor, she saw no waiting room, only a long hallway with many closed doors. Rene stood in front of a door and opened it with his keys. Natalie was looking down the hall with concern.

"Come in Natalie, I won't do anything to you."

She entered and noticed René's apartment was only one room; no kitchen or bathroom were visible. There was one bed, a table and a chair. She figured he didn't have a private bathroom because there was only one small sink and a towel hanging on a nail. She didn't say anything, but René understood by her expression that she didn't like his place.

"Don't you like this?"

"Well, it's good for one person only, but not for a family."

"Yes, but they have bigger apartments. I can talk to the owner, I know him, so he can rent one to you for a good price."

"Thanks René, I appreciate your interest, but I won't live here. I have to go now. I will take a taxi to take me home, you don't have to give me a ride."

When she finished talking, she made a motion to leave, but the man closed the door with a quick move and put his back against it to stop her from leaving.

"What are you doing René? You cannot stop me from leaving."

She turned pale and for the first time understood that he had planned everything to trap her. She had been very naive believing in his words. He didn't have a car, he was not showing her his apartment and he was not trying to help her. He had clearly other intentions.

"Open the door Rene, you don't think that because you gave me a job I am going to stay with you here."

Then he hugged her with his strong arms and tried to kiss her, but she resisted with all her strength, pushing him away with her arms.

"Leave me alone Rene, you don't know me. If you insist in this harassment I will scream very loud!"

Then he let go of her, but he didn't move away from the door. He was furious; his bloodshot eyes terrified her.

"Don't be crazy, if you scream it will be bad for me. I don't want to hurt you. I like you, and we can be friends."

"You don't know me, it's the first time you talked to me. How dare you bring me here with false words? Everything you told me was a lie. I am a decent woman, do you understand? Not like the ones you see on the streets."

"But, what happened? Why don't you want to stay with me? I am a good looking man, clean and a good worker, I can help you with your children."

"Shut up and let me go. I hate a liar."

He tried to hug her again, and she screamed very loud. He was enraged and threw her on the bed. She got off the bed very quickly and ran to open the window.

"I will scream again if you touch me and now somebody will hear, and the police will come."

René's face was very red, his eyes red with anger. But when he saw her determination he changed his attitude, trying to win her confidence again.

"Please Natalie don't make a scene here, it's not necessary."

She looked at him trying to appear strong and determined, hiding her fear.

"I am going to do it if you don't let me go."

"Give me a chance girl, I like you very much, and I am a lonely man, I don't have anybody as you can see."

He came back to try and hug her, but she resisted again.

"I am sorry René, that's not how you are going to get a woman like me. You have to respect me. You made a mistake. I am not an easy woman, like you think."

"But you look like one."

"Why? What is wrong with my appearance that you treat me like this?"

"Nothing but it is just the way you dress and the way you walk, everything is very provocative."

"You don't know what you are saying. In my country they would not talk to a decent woman like you did."

He was laughing now listening to her words.

"So you think you are a distinguish woman, and you are looking for a waitress job? I laugh at this. Who knows where you came from, and want to look like you are very important? You are very proud, but you are nothing. You are not worth ten dollars. I have many women that want me, true woman, not like you pale and skinny."

She didn't pay attention to his angry words and grabbed her purse and packages and walked in the direction of the door. She was shaking because that man could stop her again. If he forced her, she would not be able to fight back. Finally, after what seemed to be the longest walk of her life, she reached the door. She opened it and left running down the long, silent hallway. Her steps sounded hard and loud on the old carpeting. She continued down the endless stairs and finally caught her breath when she reached the lobby.

She tried to regain her composure and managed to look back to see if he was following her; he was not. Natalie went out to the lonely streets and waited for a taxi, her heart beating rapidly, trying to grapple with what had just happened. After a few minutes, a taxi passed by and she got in it. When the taxi was leaving she looked up towards René's apartment and saw him at the window watching her, but now he was harmless. She had ten dollars in her purse, enough to get her downtown. The tips she had forgotten in the restaurant.

That night was the worst experience of her life. She thanked God for helping her. Natalie felt the refreshing the wind as the cab crossed the causeway over the bay, back to her apartment downtown. She felt happy and relieved to have escaped from that man. Now the problems with Maria seem insignificant compared with what she has just gone through. A stranger had intended to rape her, and she was so naïve she was not able to see it coming. She arrived to her apartment, opened the door and she felt very happy. Her children were sleeping peacefully. She whispered:

"Thank you God, I will never trust a stranger again."

CHAPTER 5

WRONG SIGNAL

NEXT MORNING NATALIE ARRIVED EARLY at Jose's Restaurant. Jose still hadn't opened but he was already inside. She waited for a moment. Jose saw her and opened the door. The regular customers were waiting outside. It was 5:50 am and he was not ready for them. When Natalie entered the cafeteria she was surprised to see another woman there in a white uniform, preparing the coffee for the customers.

"Good morning." Natalie said.

The woman returned her greetings. She was older than Natalie, probably in her early forties, well groomed and hair tinted in a blondish color. Natalie noticed that she had been to the beauty parlor and took good care of her appearance.

Natalie sat close to the counter and she didn't go to the kitchen to avoid talking to Maria. She didn't do anything to try to help because she didn't know if she still had a job. The woman brought her coffee. She was obviously not aware that Natalie worked there; apparently Jose hadn't said anything about her. Trying to appear calm, she started drinking her coffee. She was waiting for Jose to tell her something. A few minutes passed and Natalie saw Nohemi go into the kitchen. Natalie overheard the conversation:

"Did you see Felicia?" Maria said.

"She is going to start working again today."

"But, they told me she was sick."

"No, she is good, thank God. Now we can work alright because she is the best."

"And me, Maria, am I not good enough?" Nohemi asked.

"You are average, you loose a lot of time talking to costumers."

"Listen Maria, don't start with me. I make everything good. Don't think that I am like Natalie that ignores everything you tell her. I am an Indian, you know, and from Honduras so you better be careful with me."

Nohemi's voice sounded loud, and Jose, who was working finishing up the tables and setting the temperature for the air conditioner, heard them and went to kitchen. Maria was now trying to be conciliatory with Nohemi:

"But, I was only playing with you. I know that you work well, not like the other."

Then, she heard Jose's voice:

"Maria it's too early to argue, people are waiting and we need the sales."

"But I didn't say anything against her, this girl doesn't understand what I said."

"Are you saying that I am stupid?" Nohemi replied.

"Please Nohemi, look for your apron, and go to the dinning room, I am going to open now, and I don't want any problems."

"Listen Jose," Nohemi said. "What do you want to do with Natalie? She is over there waiting."

I know, I will talk with her, don't you worry."

"Don't leave her without a job, she has four kids."

Jose went to open the door, and the costumers streamed in like usual, trying to get the best seats. Some of them said hello to Natalie who was still sitting in the same place. She finished drinking her coffee, and started playing with the teaspoon. She felt awkward because she didn't have to wait on anybody, and was sitting down like any other customer. The conversation she heard inside the kitchen was a bad sign for her. She was loosing hope; she may not have a job. Suddenly she felt tired, sleepy, and without any wish to talk or discuss anything with anybody. Felicia, the woman who Maria liked so much, was nice and she asked her if she wanted to eat breakfast. Natalie replied:

"I would like a complete breakfast, but without grits," she said in Spanish.

At that moment she felt good to be served because it reminded her of the time when she sat at the table in her house, and the servant would ask her what she wanted for breakfast. Her thoughts flew back instinctively to better times, and she took refuge in her past life as a way to resist the present reality. For a moment she was far away from the restaurant. Her dinner table was simple, but clean, with white tablecloth and good china. She remembered the pitcher of coffee, the fine cups, the hot bread, and the glasses with the orange juice for her and the children. They were always in a hurry to take the bus to school. Rosa liked fried eggs and Maria scrambled. Adrian preferred hard-boiled, as did Eugenia. The morning was fresh, and she could see from the open window in the dinning room the green grass wet from the morning dew. She liked to watch the big tree at the entrance to the garden, close to the fence painted brown. It was the windy season, a pleasant time of the year. The dry leaves were falling and flying away dispersed by the morning breeze; then they disappeared in the distance. The servant didn't like the tree because she had to pick up the leaves every morning. But Natalie loved the tree and the birds that flew between the branches. It was a strong banyan tree. The children made swings and hung them there; it was their favorite spot in the yard. However, the owner of the house wanted to cut it down because the roots could destroy the foundation of the house. She didn't understand how important the tree was for Natalie's family or that the shade of the tree in a torrid climate sheltered the house from the scorching sun. But her tree was still in the garden, and Natalie enjoyed while eating breakfast every morning.

Felicia's voice brought her back to her reality in the US. She heard Felicia telling her that her breakfast was getting cold. Natalie looked at her and the magic was broken. Her table by the window with the yellow curtains moving with the ocean breeze disappeared. She was in a very different place; she looked around and saw hungry men devouring messy fried eggs with grits, and paying little attention to basic table manners.

"Thank you Felicia, breakfast is delicious."

She intended to eat, but she lost her appetite. She drank the orange juice and put the butter on the bread. At this moment, Irma entered the restaurant with her daughter. She was well dressed like usual, and her ten-year-old daughter, Nancy, was dressed in a school's uniform, carrying her schoolbooks. Jose came from the kitchen when he heard Irma's voice, and asked,

"Why are you here so early today?"

"Well, Nancy missed the bus, and I have to take her to school. She woke up late because she was watching TV until I don't know what time."

She was obviously angry with Nancy and told her:

"If this happens again you would stay home because I go to bed very late and I am tired, and I shouldn't have to wake up early."

"I can take her." Jose said.

"That is not the point, it's not good, and this is the reason she does that. You accept everything Nancy does. You don't help me educate her."

Jose didn't answer, and went back to finish the job he was doing.

Then Irma said hello to Felicia and hugged her. It seemed like everybody appreciated her. Natalie looked at all of them and thought that it would be nice if somebody appreciated her for what she was. While Nancy was eating her breakfast, Irma sat next to Natalie and explained:

"Yesterday I was calling to tell you not to come to work in the morning, but you weren't at home. Your friend Margarita told me that you would come back later. I don't know where you were. I tried two times, but it was impossible to talk with you."

"Well, I was in Miami Beach, looking for some clothes for my children."

"In Miami Beach? Here you can get everything; you don't have to go so far, taking buses and spending extra money."

"Yes, but sometimes I like to change ambience."

"Anyway, you are here. Do you know Felicia? She has been working with us a long time, and she worked the first shift. She is going to work with Nohemi. You will work the second shift with Luisa; she is a very good girl and works fast. You won't have any problem because work at night it is easier, not like in the morning, and you will get more tips. Besides, I will be here to help and Roberta, the cook, is the best."

She said this in a low voice to keep Maria out of it.

Natalie felt a little better hearing that she still had a job, but the shift was not good for her children. She told Irma about that, but she didn't give her any other option. Jose told her from the beginning that Natalie had to work the second shift when Felicia came back. Natalie had to conform to the owner's decision and told Irma she would come back at three o'clock. At least she wouldn't have to work with Maria. She hoped Roberta had a better personality.

She left the restaurant and returned home to cook something for the children, and to write a note telling them about the new shift. Her shift would finish at eleven o'clock. They lived close to the restaurant and she could arrive quickly. After she prepared dinner for the children, she remembered that the electricity bill had to be paid. The office was very close, and she had time to go before the start of her new shift. While she was walking, her mind was wondering about working the second shift. Irma said she would be there to help, but she was meticulous about costumer service, and she became impatient very easily if service was not done promptly and correctly.

By the time she arrived, she had already forgotten about the restaurant, Maria and the new shift. She had turned her attention to other things. Natalie paid seven dollars for the electricity, which was not much because they didn't have air conditioning, and electricity was cheap. It was lunchtime and Natalie decided to go to an American cafeteria she knew where they served great soups. The place was full. She lined up for a while, bought soup, salad and coffee, and started looking for a table with the tray in her hands. She couldn't find any place to sit. She felt uncomfortable because people were looking at her, walking from one place to another. Finally a man who had been watching her asked her to sit at his table.

"You can sit here, I only need one seat."

"Thanks, but I don't want to bother you."

"It's not a problem, you can sit down."

"Oh, thank you, this place it's so full at this time."

"Yes, it is."

She sat down in front of the man. He was a young American man and good looking. She noticed he looked like he worked at an office or a bank because he wore an elegant suit, dark blue with a red tie. Natalie didn't look at him anymore, and she started to eat her soup and salad that was very delicious. Natalie finished eating and started to put sugar in her coffee when he started a conversation.

"Excuse me," he said in English. "Where are you from?"

She looked at him; he had blue eyes, with a sweet look. She answered, but didn't tell him the truth.

"I am a tourist. I'm here for a week."

"But you speak English well." He said smiling.

Natalie noticed when he smiled that his teeth were white and his smile attractive. She felt the urge to leave. She didn't want to make any friends, especially a handsome and elegant man like him. But suddenly Natalie felt a desperate need to speak English well and have a conversation with him like a young American girl, talking fluently without having to think about every word. She wanted to break the worst barrier between the two civilizations. Then she smiled and her face changed. The man looked at her like she was a different woman, probably her smile was very attractive, or she showed more personality. While he was looking at her she was thinking:

"If I could be an American like him, we could talk on equal ground and maybe he would invite me to a very elegant place, and I would have a pretty dress like Cinderella. He would pick me up in a new car, and bring me flowers. He would open the car door, and he almost wouldn't recognize me in my beautiful dress. Then we would go to dinner, and he would order champagne or maybe wine."

The man made a sound with the glass of water and Natalie suddenly woke up to reality. She smiled, but now as the real Natalie, the immigrant, the restaurant waitress and mother of four children. It was her only reality. Then she said:

"I would like to speak good English, but it's difficult. I have been studying in my country, but I would like to practice here, to go to the college."

"But there is a college around here, you can get a student Visa."

"I know. Some day I will do it, for now it's impossible."

"What is your hotel?" He asked changing the conversation.

"Nearby." But she didn't say the name.

"I see you don't want to tell me where you live. It's okay, but you can tell me your name?"

"Yes, my name is Natalie."

"Oh that is a beautiful name."

At that moment, she saw he had something in his hand, she noticed it was money. She thought it was a dollar for the tip. But he kept playing with the bill, while he looked at her directly with insistence. Natalie was surprised to see a one-hundred-dollar bill. Natalie's eyes followed the movement of his hand, folding and unfolding the bill, insinuating something, while his green's eyes observed her. Then she understood the man's intentions. She felt so appalled that she couldn't say a thing. The coffee forgotten, she watched the bill that had the same color of his eye. No flowers, no champagne and no Cinderella story. She didn't feel indignation, but extreme humiliation. She felt disappointed with herself for having been so naïve. Natalie stood up, grabbed her purse, but before leaving, she turned to him and said with a firm voice.

"Mr. you have made a big mistake."

She left without waiting for an answer. He didn't deserve one. She walked along the sidewalk full of people coming and going. It was a beautiful city with seemingly very rich people, but there was a selfish and brutal materialist everywhere. Only money mattered, and she suddenly understood that her sentimental nature was out of sync with her new social reality. She had to learn to be strong every minute. But would she be able to change? Will she be like Maria or other immigrants who defended themselves by cursing and fighting? Could she become one of them? She didn't know. The elegant man who she met in the restaurant seemed very nice and respectable. However, he was another René dressed in elegant cloth. Inside they were the same.

CHAPTER 6

HIUNDI

NATALIE LIKED THE AFTERNOON SHIFT because costumers were younger and left better tips. Roberta, the cook, was an affable lady who laughed, smoked and joked all the time, except when Jose was there. Natalie got along well with her. The busiest time of the day was from six to seven p.m., and Luisa and Natalie were running to serve everyone. Luisa was a young woman in her late twenties, dark skin and gracious face. She was a little silly in the way she interacted with people and made some customers smile out of pity. Irma liked her because she was fast and outgoing, always ready to tell a story of her life in New York and in other places.

Natalie learned the ropes quickly and nobody had to boss her around anymore. She made friends during that shift. Some of them were good people and she could have conversations with them. She felt less lonely now. But time passed by slowly and she was always looking at the clock that Jose had hung on the wall of the dinning room. This was not a job for her. She knew that to get a better job she needed to improve her English studying at a college. Just across the street Miami Dade Community College beaconed her. She would look with certain envy at the students who came in and out laughing and joking, carrying their book bags.

At four o'clock in the afternoon her children came to the restaurant to see her. They always did this when they left the school. It was the happiest moment of the day. She kissed them and the problems of the day seemed to dissipate. How beautiful they looked in their uniforms, books in hands. Rosa had her long blonde hair below her shoulders, her eyes telling her mother she wished to spend more time with her. Maria, always happy with smile on her face, told Natalie many things about the new friends she met.

Adrian with his big eyes was silent most of the time, but looking at her with love. Eugenia was usually absent, coming back from school later.

"You know Mami," Maria said,

"I speak English with my friends. Three of them live in Miami Beach. They want me to visit them. Can I go on Sunday?"

"Don't pay attention to her, mami," Rosa said.

"She has only known them since yesterday, and she wants to visit already?"

"It is not true Rosa, I have know them for several days. They are very good people, and we play volleyball."

Adrian was silent looking at his mother.

"What happened Adrian? You are very quiet. Are you hungry?"

"Yes" he answered. Natalie prepared sandwiches for all of them, and she paid for them at the register. Those were the only happy moments she had during afternoons at the restaurant.

Then they would leave for the apartment happy or sometimes arguing among each other over the simplest thing. "Children are like that," she thought smiling. Natalie wished she could go with them, but it was impossible. She worried about her four children being alone in the apartment. The neighbors were not bad, but she didn't know all of them. Some looked downright weird, especially "El Chino," who lived on the first floor and gave Rosa the creeps every time she saw him. The man didn't say anything to her, but Rosa was afraid of him and she always worried about him. When Natalie mentioned this to Irma she said something that gave her some hope. Jose had bought a house in a better neighborhood and maybe he would rent it to her. Irma explained,

"the house has two bedrooms, living room, dinning room, kitchen, and a porch. Also the house has a yard where Adrian can play without any danger. He can play with Nancy. "My mother lives with me and they won't feel alone. You have to pay more, but it's what you need with your children. If you want I can talk with Jose. When he finishes fixing and painting the house, you can move in."

"Oh, this would be great; are you sure?"

Natalie couldn't believe what Irma had just told her.

"I told you that you could have the house if you want to. I am going to tell Jose to rent it to you."

"It is marvelous. How much is the rent for that house?"

"I don't know yet, but let him finish, and I will talk with him about it."

Natalie was very happy and the costumers saw her smiling that afternoon. She made jokes like never before. She was always serious, but this day she was unrecognizably cheerful. That night a new costumer came to the restaurant, someone they had never seen before. He was a young Indian; brown skin, straight dark hair, and nice appearance. His white teeth contrasted with his brown skin. Luisa took care of him and she soon learned everything about him.

"He was working at a jewelry store downtown where they sell fine wristwatches. His name was Hiundi and he was single."

Luisa was very exited; she got a two-dollar tip, and she told Irma she liked him.

"He has pretty black eyes, and his skin is soft and dark." Luisa said smiling.

"Black skin I would say," Roberta expressed her opinion.

"No, he is not black, he is from India, a true Indian. Besides, he has straight hair."

"I know Luisa, but be careful because you like all men."

Irma and Roberta smiled and Luisa made a coquettish gesture with her face and body. But it was only for a moment because she didn't pay much attention to what people said about her. She then ran again to serve another promising costumer with good appearance.

Hiundi came back for dinner on another night and Luisa was quick to serve him. Luisa told him that Natalie needed a wristwatch urgently.

"She is always asking us what time it is. I am tired of it."

The young guy looked at Natalie for the first time, and he called her as she passed by with the tray in her hands after serving food to another customer. Because he was Luisa's costumer, Natalie told him she would be right back. She returned and asked him what he wanted.

"Nothing he said, but I want to talk to you."

Natalie observed his big eyes, black and sad, like she had never seen before. He looked like a legendary Indian, with an irremediable penury reflected in his eyes. She thought he was an interesting man, and quickly put her mind to rest to prevent judging him further. She had a bad augury about this man and she wanted to erase that from her mind. He talked in English with a foreign accent.

"Luisa told me that you need a wristwatch."

"Yes it's true. Do you work in a store where they sell wristwatches?"

"Yes, two blocks from here. This is the address, I am always there during the morning."

Natalie took the card and later put it in her purse.

"You know, I cannot pay a lot. Do you think maybe I can get something for around twenty dollars?"

Hiundi smiled, and he answered:

"Sure, there are all different prices."

"Then, I will go tomorrow, like Luisa said, I need a wristwatch."

Hiundi and Natalie spoke a little about the food that he liked. Natalie was very curious about his country; she was always interested in other cultures.

"It is true that the women in your country have to cover their faces to go out, and only the husband can see them?"

He smiled and nodded:

"Yes and no. This is an old tradition and we are now very modern. As a matter of fact, in some regions the women cover their head. This is a religious matter."

He asked her changing the subject:

"Are you coming tomorrow?"

"Yes, I will go at eleven o'clock."

"Okay I will wait for you. If you don't see me just ask for me, please. Your name is Natalie right?"

"Yes, and please don't forget because if I go and you don't recognize me, I am going to feel very bad."

"Why do you say that? Do I seem like a liar?"

She smiled.

"Forgive me I was kidding you."

But he was serious when he looked at her. At that moment Luisa came back and told Natalie in Spanish,

"do you want to take him for yourself?"

Natalie smiled as she moved away from Hiundi, leaving her plenty of room.

People gossiped about Luisa being pregnant, but Natalie didn't know for sure.

Maybe she is looking for a father for her child, because she doesn't have a husband or a boyfriend. Hiundi watched both and asked.

"What did she say to you?"

"Nothing, important."

Hiundi smiled again, and he took out his wallet and gave one dollar to each. After that he got up and walked towards the door. Luisa said:

"Goodbye my love."

Natalie noticed that he didn't like that, and he replied:

"Good night to all of you."

"He is a nice guy," Irma said, "He is good for Luisa."

She smiled delighted.

"Yes he is good for me, but not for Natalie because she is too old for him."

"I'm not interested in Hiundi. We were talking tonight about a watch, like you mentioned to him, remember?"

"It is true, but tonight he was looking at you in a particular way that surprised me."

"You are crazy Luisa, the poor guy doesn't even know my name, so let's not joke about it. We have to clean the floor. It is time for me to worry about my children alone in that apartment."

CHAPTER 7

NOT MY WATCH

THE JEWELRY STORE WHERE HIUNDI worked at was big with pretty showcases. Natalie could see beautiful jewelry and wristwatches. She arrived early and saw him taking care of another woman. There were two more employees and a lady at the register. When one of them offered to help her, she said:

"Thank you, I am only looking."

She observed the kind of wristwatches they had and thought they were not for her. There wasn't anything for less than fifty dollars. She hoped that the cheap watches were kept in another place. Hiundi had told her there were all kinds of watches at different prices. She waited for Hiundi more than ten minutes and finally he noticed her presence. He finished with the woman who bought an expensive wristwatch. He saw Natalie, and made a sign with his hand telling her to come closer.

"May I help you, Miss?"

He asked, simulating he didn't know her.

Natalie came close to him and told him she wanted to see some wristwatches. The other employees went to take care of other things and Hiundi was left alone with her.

He knew that she was in a serious mood and didn't say hello.

"What kind of wristwatch are you looking for?" Do you prefer any brand in particular?"

"No, I want a good wristwatch, but not too expensive, maybe you can help me."

"Sure, I will show you some you may like."

Hiundi was looked through several boxes; he looked for brand name watches, and he brought them for her to see. She looked at him for a moment, and Hiundi smiled slightly, but he was silent. Natalie noticed he didn't want people in the store to know that they were friends. She felt bad about this; probably he was embarrassed because she didn't have enough money to buy an expensive watch.

Hiundi started to open the boxes, and put in front of her several watches. They were very beautiful, especially one with a gold bracelet that seemed right for her wrist.

"Which do you like?" He asked.

"This one," she said," it's beautiful."

Then, he took her hand and put the watch on her wrist.

Natalie looked at the watch; it was so pretty that it made her look like a rich woman.

"It's pretty, perfect for me, but I imagine this watch is very expensive."

"No, it's not too expensive because it is made out of gold."

She looked at him with surprise because he knew that she couldn't pay for a wristwatch like that. She checked the price. It cost $125 dollars. She took it off very carefully and put it back on the counter. She knew now that in this store they didn't have anything she could afford.

"Thank you," she said, "I will come back tomorrow because I like this one a lot."

"Yes, you can come back tomorrow." Hiundi replied.

He started to pick up the wristwatches from the counter and putting them back in the boxes very slowly while he looked at Natalie.

"Thank you, for taking your time to show me the watches." She added.

But at that exact moment, Hiundi did the unthinkable. He took the watch she liked and slid it over the counter, covering it with his hand, and put it inside Natalie's dress pocket. She was shocked. He had put the watch inside her pocket.

"God," Natalie thought, "I have to go now; I'm an accomplice on this now."

He turned his back to the other employees, obstructing their view. Natalie was stunned for a moment, but she regained control of herself and quickly put her hand in her pocket and retrieved the expensive watch.

"Look, Mr. this is not my watch!"

He looked at her with surprise, his black eyes wide open, but after a second, he grabbed it, reached for a box and put it away. He didn't say anything or looked at her when she left.

Natalie was very scared, walking fast in the direction of the restaurant and feeling like a criminal. She recreated in her mind Hiundi's quick gesture to put the watch inside her small pocket. She didn't have good luck; everything she tried to do seemed to come out wrong. She was a good woman, not a thief, or somebody who would take money in exchange for her body.

That day in the restaurant she spoke very little and dedicated all her attention to the costumers, trying not to think of the incident with Hiundi. She can properly buy a wristwatch in any store, maybe not so beautiful. At nine o'clock as usual, Hiundi came to the restaurant. He was dressed in white and his black hair was combed very neatly. It was Luisa's day off, and Natalie served him. She said hello, discretely, without smiling, but with courtesy. He looked at her with an insistent stare, but he didn't say anything about what occurred that morning

While he was eating, Natalie went to take care of another costumer. She wanted to say something to him about the incident because what he did was very wrong. It was stealing and she would have been his accomplice, no matter what. But the people around them impeded her from saying anything. Finally, at ten o'clock the place was almost empty and Natalie approached him. His sad eyes were looking at her with interest.

"Why didn't you take the wristwatch?" He asked in a soft voice.

"Because I cannot afford it, I told you. I didn't know your store only sold very expensive wristwatches."

"How silly you are Natalie, you don't see that I wanted to give it to you."

His voice sounded passionate.

"You are crazy Hiundi, you don't see? that is stealing and they would think I am a thief and I could be in trouble with the police."

"Please, don't say anything more, I know what I did. Give me the bill, please"

She figured out his total and gave him the bill. It was five dollars.

When she extended her hand to receive the money, she noticed that there was something else under the five dollars.

"What is this?"

She asked a little worried . . . He smiled sweetly, and looking at her, said:

"It is a little gift for you."

"Wait Hiundi, come back please."

She tried to stop him, but he didn't stop, and he left in a hurry. Nobody noticed what happened between Natalie and the young guy, but Natalie was nervous for the rest of the night with the little box in her apron, which Hiundi gave her. Finally her curiosity was too strong, and she went to the bathroom to see what he gave her. She took it out of the box very delicately and started to open the little package covered with fine paper. The box was in red velvet, very soft to the touch. She opened to see what she was expecting: the same wristwatch he dropped in her pocket that morning.

"What am I going to do now?"

He had already left, but she could not keep the watch. For an instant she loved the watch and hated it at the same time. She didn't know what to do. To take the watch would probably be too compromising, and she did not want that. She was poor but free, and she liked to remain that way. She did not want any more problems.

She thought that Hiundi didn't need to do that to conquer a woman's heart. He was an attractive man, but not for her. Finally the time came to go back to her apartment. She felt scared to walk alone four blocks with that expensive watch in her purse. Sometimes Jose or a customer accompanied her to her place, but that night nobody could do it. She hid the watch in her blouse and started walking the lonely streets. As always, she prayed to God to protect her because the children needed her.

When she was almost home, a dirty man who was living on the street came close to her, but she walked quickly and crossed the street. She stopped in front of the Fire Station that was always open. A fireman who was on duty asked her if she needed some help.

"I am afraid of this man, and I need to arrive home."

The man she mentioned was hiding in a dark corner and the officer couldn't see him.

"Where are you coming from at this time?" he asked.

"From my work. It is a restaurant and they close at eleven o'clock."

"But you are not supposed to come alone around here at this time. There are always drunks and thieves around here."

"I know, but I have to work."

"If you want I will go with you. Do you live close to here?"

"Yes, in that building."

Oh, it is very close, I am going with you, it's is not a problem."

"Thank you, I appreciate that."

The fireman accompanied Natalie to her place and she felt very happy, like always, when she came back to her children.

Every day for Natalie was a struggle, one more day of fighting for survival. That day was even worse because of the problem with the watch. She looked at it closely under the light of the living room lamp.

"How beautiful it is, but tomorrow I'll give it back to Hiundi," she decided.

She had no choice. The paths that opened for her were dangerous. She couldn't take this seemingly easy path, which was contrary to the idea she had when she made the decision to abandon her country. Her children came first before anything else in her life, and she had to remain strong in her belief, no matter how many interesting men will appear in her life. Probably some day she will find someone who would come to her with a clean, honest mind, and they will find true love. It may be difficult, but she would wait for him. She thought again of Hiundi, and felt sorry for him. What he was doing was wrong, dishonest and dangerous. He could be caught. Maybe he did the same thing with other women.

It was cold the next morning, and a mantle of grey clouds covered the clear blue sky that made Miami a tropical paradise. The sun appeared shy and unable to penetrate the gray clouds. Miami lost its magic appearance and was turned into a cold, grey city overnight. Once again, people in colorful coats, sweaters and hats inundated the city.

"Another cold front; it is going to be cold for the next three days," was the comment of the day on the street.

Winter in South Florida was a wonderful time of balmy and clear weather interrupted occasionally by a cold spell that sent people indoors. By now, Natalie and her children were accustomed to these changes. The children went to school very proud with their coats and dark blue berets. Adrian didn't like wearing that, but his mother explained that it was necessary to protect him against the cold, otherwise he could get sick. The boy understood and went to school with his two sisters. She looked at them from her window on the third floor and she smiled cheerfully. God was good to her because they were in good health, especially during unexpected the cold weather of forty degrees. The apartment was cold because they didn't have a heater. Natalie sat on the sofa covered with a blanket and tried to distract herself by watching the black-and-white television they had bought. She liked watching TV in English because it helped her understand the language that was so difficult for her. She tried to concentrate but to no avail, her thoughts went irremediably to Hiundi. What was she going to do when he comes back to the restaurant that night?

CHAPTER 8

A FAREWELL

NATALIE HAD ALREADY MADE HER decision, but her thoughts kept coming back over and over again. What would he say about her returning the wristwatch? That she was a silly girl who didn't accept a gift she wished for and needed? Maybe he would think she is returning it because it is not longer in style. He would probably never understand the real reason why she is doing that, and will not be able to convince him about her decision. It is going to be a futile effort. Hiundi belonged to a different world and there was no room for Natalie there.

When she thought about that, she stood up and the blanket slid to the floor. Natalie decided to go out for some fresh air. She was supposed to be enjoying her time off and not thinking about any more problems. She then left the apartment to take a walk out on the street. She wanted to see happy people despite of the cold weather. Her coat wasn't elegant, but it protected her well from the frigid wind that funneled through the high rises, picking up speed as it passed through Downtown Miami. The wind played with the dried leaves from the trees, blowing them away along with the dirty papers and newspapers that the people let behind on the benches of Bayfront Park. The winter changed everything around and Natalie loved it. She could sense it in the air. Smelling in the cold wind, she could taste the mountain air from a faraway place in the north. Each breath of clean fresh air was like a jolt of energy, the smell of a less civilized world. She breathed in the cold air and her body shivered, but she felt better, less lonely and more hopeful. She walked up to the "Pigeons Park" and sat on one of the bench to see the countless pigeons eating the breadcrumbs that someone had thrown on the ground. On her days off, she sometimes brought her children to the park, which they loved, especially playing with the pigeons.

It was ten o'clock and the sun came out timidly from behind the clouds, heating up the morning. It was warming rapidly and the temperature was probably reaching sixty degrees Fahrenheit because her hands weren't cold anymore. She looked around and saw few people walking in the park, which was normal on a cold morning when most people preferred to remain indoors perhaps drinking coffee.

Natalie got up from the bench and started walking in the center of the park, surrounded by tropical plants and big trees. She liked everything, especially Biscayne Bay, glittering in the background. She thought that it was the most beautiful thing in Miami. She sat down again and the sunlight became incredibly bright, penetrating deep into the turquoise waters of the bay. She whished she could spend more time there, looking at the ducks swimming and the seaweed entwined in the rocks of the bay. She remained there for some time deeply immersed in the magic of the moment.

"Natalie, what are you doing here all alone?"

She was suddenly awakened from her daydreaming by a voice in English. She was startled, and looked towards the voice. It was a young man, and under the morning light he appeared even younger. He was dressed in a blue sweeter and black pant, and he wore dark sunglasses. It was Hiundi. For a moment she was confused because she didn't expect to see him there.

"Hello Hiundi, you scared me."

"Yes, I noticed that. You looked at me like I was another person."

No, I was only distracted, looking at the beautiful view I can see from here."

"Do you like the sea?"

"Oh yes, I love it."

"You are very romantic Natalie. I saw you when you passed by my store, and I thought at lunch time about coming here to talk to you."

"Yes, I think we should. Last night you gave me something that you know I cannot accept."

"Why not?"

Hiundi sat down close to her and looked at her.

"Because I cannot pay for this in any form."

When she said that, she looked away trying not to see his eyes, which looked at her persistently.

"I told you it's a gift, you don't have to pay anything."

"I am sorry Hiundi, I am going to give it back to you tonight. It is better you take it back to the store."

He moved his head negatively.

"This is my problem, and I will pay for it. It is you that I am worried about. You are a very strange woman. You are lonely, and yet you don't want any company. Why Natalie?" He insisted, "I like you a lot because you are sweet and so pretty."

"You are younger than me."

She answered a little confused because of his closeness.

Hiundi looked at her with surprise.

"Is this what you worry about? This is not important to me, I like you the way you are."

After he said that, he tried to hug and kiss her, but Natalie quickly moved to the other side of the bench, pushing him away. He didn't insist and said:

"I thought you liked me a little."

"Yes I like you, but only as a friend. Do you know Hiundi? Luisa likes you."

"I know, but I don't like her, Luisa is dirty and talks too much. I don't like that kind of women."

They both were silent for a moment, watching the ducks swimming by.

"How many children do you have, Natalie?"

"Four, three girls and a boy."

He took Natalie's hand and caressed it.

"You know, I don't like to see you work so hard in that place, it is damaging your hands, look how they are, and that woman in the kitchen is so bad, always after you, pushing you to work harder. I would like to help you with your children. We can see each other for a while, and it is possible that you may learn to love me a little. I could be happy with a woman like you."

She was silent and didn't look at him. He was talking in a soft manner, and the touch of his hand was gentle. For an instant she wanted to put her head on his shoulder and rest a bit. His clothes were clean and he smelled of cologne. It was a day when one person needed another. The young man at her side, the gold wristwatch that could be hers, but then she remembered her children, and everything fell into place again.

"I can't Hiundi, I cannot." She said.

"Why not?"

He insisted on kissing her face. Natalie felt some emotion, but she didn't respond to his caresses.

"Leave me alone please Hiundi, we are different, I know that this relationship won't be good."

"Don't you want to try?"

He asked with a soft voice close to her ear.

"I will be the most faithful Man, I swear to God."

"No Hiundi, don't swear, it's not necessary, understand, I am older than you; I am thirty four years old, and you are only twenty five."

"I am twenty seven years old, but I don't see why it is so important to you."

"Because I have advanced a lot in my life and you are only starting."

He laughed.

"Do you believe that? If you knew how much I have lived, and all I know, you would be surprised. I could be your teacher. Give me a kiss Natalie, you are so beautiful, I love you very much."

Hiundi hugged her, and she felt the heat of his body, young and clean. For a moment she let him hug her. His arms were strong, but didn't imprison her. His black eyes looked close, and Natalie could see a passionate light in them. He tried to kiss her on the lips, but she refused.

"No Hiundi please, leave me alone."

He tried again and kissed her, but she didn't respond to his caress. Then Hiundi let her go without insisting anymore.

Two days later, Hiundi came back to the restaurant. Luisa smiled and went quickly to serve him. But he didn't look at her; his voice was cold when he told her what he wanted to eat. He started to read a newspaper he brought. Natalie was on the other side of the counter and pretended she didn't see him. She still had the wristwatch, but she didn't have it that night because he missed two days coming to the restaurant. At some point when she passed close to him, he said:

"Natalie please, can you bring me a cup of coffee?"

"Sure Hiundi,"

She answered smiling casually. Luisa didn't like this, and looked at her disappointed.

"You know that I was taking care of him."

"Yes, but he called me."

"I see, if you want to take him, do it, for me it is the same. I don't care."

She turned her back on him with a bad attitude and started to talk to another costumer. When the bell in the kitchen rang, indicating Hiundi's order was ready, Luisa didn't go to take it and Natalie had to do it. Hiundi observed everything that was happening, but he didn't say a thing. He started to eat slowly pretending he didn't notice what happened between the two girls. Luisa was jealous, and demonstrated her emotion in a bad way. When he asked for his bill, Irma had to call Luisa to bring it. Natalie didn't pay attention to Luisa's attitude, and she went ahead with the same routine, serving her costumers who were now friendly with her because she was fast and efficient.

Hiundi didn't come back after the incident with Luisa. Later next Saturday, he entered the restaurant without saying hello to anybody. Luisa tried to establish a conversation, but he ignored her. He called Natalie instead. Luisa looked at Natalie very angrily. When Natalie was close to him, Hiundi asked her in a soft voice:

"Did you change your opinion about me?"

Natalie was writing his order, and pretended she didn't hear because Luisa was close. She went to the kitchen to enter the order. She then got her purse, opened it, and took the little box that contained the wristwatch. Tonight, she had to give it back and he probably won't come back again. Natalie felt bad when she realized this, and suddenly she knew that she would miss him, but she cannot complicate her life further. She had just arrived in this country, leaving everything behind to look for peace and liberty. She knew that if she took a different path, like a love relationship with Hiundi, her future would not be good. She didn't know anything about him, and she sensed that this relationship would never be stable.

She came back and looked to see if Luisa was close to him, but she had gone out to make a phone call. Then she walked up to him and without hesitation handed him the little packet with the wristwatch. He looked at her and his eyes were sad. He took it, and put it in his pocket.

"You want to do this, Natalie? We could be very happy together."

"I know, but like I said before, my responsibility is very big, and I don't have to share it with you."

"I could do it, I told you."

She moved her head negatively.

"Thank you Hiundi, you are my friend, always I will remember you."

Luisa came back at that moment, and saw them talking in soft voices. There was hatred in her dark eyes, but she didn't say anything. Then Hiundi left saying:

"Good night to everyone"

Natalie was looking at him when he left. He was skinny with a wide back and strong body. He walked fast and disappeared in the darkness of the lonely street.

That night, Natalie went to sleep later than usual. It was four o'clock and she was still awake. Finally she fell asleep and dreamed with Hiundi who never came back to see her.

CHAPTER 9

THE HOUSE

JOSE RENTED THE HOUSE TO Natalie. The house was situated in a good residential neighborhood in North Miami. Her life changed radically with her new home. Her children were happy to be able to play outside in a real residential neighborhood with parks and green spaces. Irma and Jose lived nearby. Natalie was very happy, more than she had ever been since she arrived in the United States. The house was like a miracle for her. It had a living room, dining room, kitchen, two bedrooms, a porch and a backyard. It was even furnished since the previous owner sold it to Jose with everything in it. The front yard had a garden with a big oak tree in the middle, which reminded Natalie of her house back in her country.

The day they moved in, Eugenia, Rosa and Maria were very happy hanging curtains in the windows and putting their clothes in their own closet. Adrian was happy too, looking at the yard where he could play football, and pitch the tent Santa Claus brought him for Christmas. Natalie prayed, giving thanks to God to allow them to have such a wonderful house. The only problem was the bus that the children had to take early in the morning to go to school. It would take them an hour to get to school in a public bus. Irma loved the girls and invited them to play with Nancy in the park close to the house.

That day everything was joy. After they came back from the park, Natalie cooked chicken with rice for the children. She didn't know how to cook very well, but on this occasion it came out really good. They sat down around the table adorned with a white tablecloth and flowers Maria brought from the garden. It was the first time the family sat together to eat dinner, and everybody had a smile on their face.

But their happiness was short lived. That night temperatures plunged into the low 30s, and the house did not have any heating or effective insulation against the cold. Natalie could not remember having been so cold in her entire life. She couldn't sleep all night despite all the blankets she was able to get. Her hands and feet were numbed. Adrian cried a little because he was cold too. Only the girls seemed to have slept thanks to the heavy blankets. Natalie couldn't take it any more. Early in the morning she woke up, went to the kitchen and turned on the oven to generate some heat. She then left the door of the oven open to heat up the house. She lay down on the living-room sofa trying to sleep a little. But she couldn't stop thinking how dangerous that could be; the red-hot open oven could easily start a fire. This is how Natalie spent her first night in the new house. At six o'clock the children woke up, and found her preparing breakfast for all of them.

"Good morning mami, did you sleep good?" Rosa asked.

"No Rosa, I didn't sleep all night. It was too cold. Today I will buy two heaters one for each room. It is impossible to sleep without heaters."

"Yes, the temperature is now 35 degrees. I heard that on the radio. We have to bundle up before we walk to the bus stop."

"Yes, dear, take care of your sister and brother. You know that I cannot. I have to do many things, prepare your food and have it ready for tonight; then I have to take the bus to start work at the restaurant at three o'clock and most likely I will come back at one o'clock with Jose. I have to wait for him to bring me home."

Rosa's face looked sad to hear her mother.

"Why mami, do you have to come back so late?"

"What am I supposed to do? He finishes at eleven, and then he has to count the money in the register and check all the receipts. I know this takes time. Plus the trip here takes almost an hour. I don't like to come late, and I will try to get another job, but for now we have no choice. I will prepare the food, and all you have to do is to heat it up and serve it to all of you. But be careful with the stove, and make sure Adrian eats his dinner, you know he gets distracted."

"Yes, and he doesn't like to do his homework, and Maria also."

"I know, but they have to do it. I pay for that school through a lot of sacrifice. Remember Rosa, when you leave the school please do not forget to stop at the restaurant because I want to see all of you, please don't forget."

She repeated.

"Yes mami, I like to go there to see you, but you know, I wouldn't like to find el Chino again."

Natalie looked at her puzzled, surprised that the girl still remembered the man.

"What happened with him? Are you afraid? Did he say something bad to you?"

"No, it was that day I found him on the first floor and he told me he had a girl in China and he would like me to be his daughter. Do you think he means that he wanted to marry me?"

Then, Natalie kissed her face, and said:

"No, dear I think he was joking, or probably he has a daughter he misses very much. But don't worry, you are not going to find him again."

"I hope not, because I don't like him."

The girl left the room a little happier, calling Maria and Adrian, and forgot about the man who for some reason upset her. Natalie thought about Rosa and el chino, and she felt very good about moving far from the Downtown apartment. She had to pay more, but it minimized the dangers posed by strangers to her children. That afternoon, Natalie walked to the corner and took the bus that passed every hour. It was two o'clock when she arrived at the restaurant. Maria was still there, and she said hello to her with an indifferent tone, like usual. Jose was there too. When he saw Natalie, he asked:

"How was your first night in the house?"

"Very bad, I couldn't sleep with the cold. I have to buy two heaters. Can you give pay me one week in advance so I can buy them? I have to go now to the store; last night was terrible."

"That was because the house was empty, but later it is going to get better. I'll give the money that you need for those heaters."

"Thanks Jose, I think fifty dollars is going to be enough."

The man gave Natalie the money, and she left quickly to the closest store where they sold heaters.

"I will come back in half an hour."

"Yes, remember that your shift starts at three thirty."

Maria said from the kitchen. Natalie knew that, and she didn't have to remind her, but that woman always found a way to bother her. Natalie didn't pay attention to her words; she just smiled and walked away with elegant steps. To forget her, she thought of her nice new house and how happy her children will be. The air was cold and the wind blew her hair uncontrollably, but she was happy and stronger than before. It was one more step in the right direction, out of the labyrinth of a big country.

CHAPTER 10

JEALOUSY

TIME WENT BY FAST. NATALIE'S children adjusted well to their new life in a residential neighborhood. They took the public bus every morning to their school downtown, making friends along the way, especially Maria, who had the remarkable ability to make friends with every smile. Young and old, white and black, they all succumbed to Maria's friendliness. Maria managed to turn the long and crowded bus ride every morning into a delightful opportunity to laugh and meet people; Rosa and Adrian just played along. Eugenia was particularly happy with the new neighborhood since her school was within walking distance from the new house, and thus was spared of the long bus ride.

They enjoyed their new home too and Natalie was happy for them. But she was working harder than before, going to bed at one thirty in the morning, and waking up at six to fix breakfast for the children. Often she didn't fall asleep until three o'clock in the morning, thinking about the bills she had to pay. Rosa tried to help her:

"You don't have to wake up so early mami, you should sleep a little more. I can take care of Adrian, he only eats cereal, and Maria has scrambled eggs, and I can do all that."

"Yes dear, but when would I see you? I come back late and I find all of you asleep"

She turned very sad suddenly. The girl looked at her with her big brown, clear eyes, and Natalie knew that Rosa understood her problems. She had grown up overnight. She was no longer the playful happy girl who arrived from her country a few months before. Natalie's heart felt discouraged. She thought that maybe she had made a mistake bringing the children to the Unites States. They were still very young children who now had to accept responsibility beyond their age.

"What happened mami, why do you look at me that way?"

Natalie smiled and caressed her daughter's blond hair.

"It's nothing only that you have grown up, it could be the change in climate."

"Yes, all of my dresses are too small for me now."

"Listen Rosa do you like it here? Are you happy?"

She looked surprised at her mother.

"Yes mami, I am very happy, I can almost speak English now. You know, the teacher will give me an award for being the best in Science. This is a difficult class, but I always have good grades. She is going to mention me at the parents meeting this month. Can you go that day?"

"Oh yes, of course I can. I will be very proud of you. You only have to tell me which day and I will be there."

Natalie continued working at the restaurant without any problems with the costumers. She was nice and faster than before and her costumers had learned to finally appreciate her. The problems with Luisa, however, were getting worse. She didn't talk to Natalie except when it was necessary, and when she did, she was very cold, and sometimes rude. It became difficult to work with somebody like that, but Natalie chose to ignore her. At nine o'clock, the time that Hiundi generally arrived to the restaurant, Luisa looked out the window to the street, as if waiting for him, but the days passed by and Hiundi didn't come back.

One night, when the restaurant was empty, Luisa confronted Natalie, and told her with fury in her voice:

"You know, one day you will pay me for what you did."

Natalie looked at her with a surprised look on her face.

"What are you talking about?"

"You know what I mean."

"No, I didn't think you were serious."

"I swear to God, that you will pay me."

"But what did I do to you? I don't understand."

"You know perfectly well what you did, I lost Hiundi because of you. You took him away from me with your little face of *mosquita muerta* (dead fly), for nothing because you left him. Do you see, he hasn't returned here? It is your fault, because I am sure if you hadn't come between us I would have him now."

60

She looked at Natalie with hate, and she understood she now had a dangerous enemy because she was ignorant and revengeful. She tried to explain.

"Please Luisa, you are wrong. I never had anything with Hiundi; if he doesn't come back it is not my fault. I didn't have anything to do with it."

"Yes, you did. Somebody saw you in the Pigeons' Park hugging. You cannot refute that."

She finished in a high voice. Then Natalie got angry and answered:

"Don't scream at me Luisa. It is better to let this problem out. I can do whatever I want. If you are interested in Hiundi I give him to you. Go where he is working, you don't have to wait for him to come here. It is not my fault if he doesn't come here. Remember, the last time Hiundi was here you were indifferent and jealous. He doesn't like that kind of thing. He is a serious man and for this reason we don't see him any more. Forget about me and look for him yourself."

Luisa was taken aback by Natalie's strong words. But Natalie's attitude made her even more furious, and she slammed the counter with her fist.

"You don't send me to any place! Do you understand? I went to see him, and he didn't look at me, as if I were a dog. I can swear you told him something bad about me, but you are going to pay for sure. Nobody takes a man away from me, unless I want it!"

Luisa concluded angrily.

At that moment somebody entered the restaurant, and Natalie went to serve him, leaving the dispute for later. She planned to tell Irma what happened the next day.

But Natalie didn't have to do that. Luisa inexplicably changed her attitude toward her. She didn't see Natalie as an enemy anymore, and she seemed to forget Hiundi. She didn't mention him anymore, and she turned her attention toward some sailors who arrived at the port on weekends, and went to the restaurant to drink beer. They left her good tips. Natalie stayed away from them because she didn't want any more problems with Luisa.

One night, when Luisa was counting the tip money, she laughed and told Natalie:

"I have twice as much as you. Now it is a reality, I can buy my own car, and I don't have to take the stupid buses. I told you, now is going to be my lucky time."

"Very good,"

Natalie answered, and didn't make any more comment about it. She knew the volatile personality of the woman.

The sailors continued visiting the restaurant, drinking beer, often until Jose closed. There was one particular good-looking sailor who talked a lot to Luisa and sometimes they left together after closing time. Natalie felt better about the change in Luisa's behavior. She didn't like arguing with her over something that was not really her fault.

CHAPTER 11

LUISA'S ENIGMA

JOSE WAS DISAPPOINTED WITH LUISA'S behavior; she was spending too much time with the sailors and missing many days of work. He talked to Irma about this, but she asked him to give her another opportunity because the girl was pregnant.

"But I cannot accept that she comes in when she wants. She is only interested in working on weekends to serve the sailors, you know. Irma I don't like this situation, we have to get rid of her."

"Wait Jose, I will talk to Luisa about this. We cannot solve the problem like this. It is true that she waits on the sailors, but we do a lot of good business with them."

"I don't know," he said unconvinced, "I will give her one more week, she has to comply with her shift."

The next day after this conversation, Luisa came back to work, but she surprised everybody with her appearance. She had a new dress, expensive shoes, and a stylish hairdo that made her look stunning. She didn't look anything like neglected Luisa everybody was used to seeing. Irma was impressed:

"Luisa, you are very elegant; you look like another woman."

She laughed and showed her hand to Irma—embellished by a glittering gold ring.

"This is nothing," she added. "I bought a car; that's why I wasn't able to work those days, because I was doing all these things, insurance, signing papers, you know . . ."

"But tell me, how did you get all these?"

"Well, I have an aunt in New York that has money, and sometimes she sends some to me. I am not a poor woman like others think."

When she said that she looked at Natalie to see if she was listening, but without interrupting the conversation. Irma called Roberta who was in the kitchen to see the new Luisa. When she came to the dining area, Irma said:

"What do you think? She surprised us. She is like Cinderella,"

"I am sure she has a fairy godmother."

Luisa was in heaven, laughing out loud. She started talking with Irma about her new car, and they both went outside to see it.

"It is a beautiful red car, and it is brand new!"

Irma announced to the entire restaurant when she came back.

"I can't believe this girl, she must have won the lottery."

She became the talk of the night. For the rest of the night all they talked about was how Luisa had changed, the new car, the things she bought, and all the possibilities she will have. Jose arrived at eleven o'clock like usual, and Irma told him all about Luisa. He didn't say a thing, only smiled in disbelief about Luisa's sudden prosperity. He clearly didn't share Irma's cheerfulness. Luisa's transformation surprised the regular costumers too, and she felt very proud being the center of attention. She was talking to her friends and favorite customers, neglecting his job and leaving most of the work to Natalie. Natalie complained to Jose because she couldn't take care of everybody. Jose reminded Luisa of her duties, but she made a gesture with her shoulders and continued serving only the costumers she liked.

From here on, Natalie started noticing something unusual. Around ten o'clock, before Jose arrived, a different type of men started to frequent the restaurant: well dressed, secretive and evasive—the kind of people never seen in the restaurant before. They ordered coffee or beer from Luisa, and she went out of her way to serve them. In return, she received generous tips, unheard of at the restaurant. When Jose arrived at eleven at night to close, the men left immediately. Natalie noticed that they were quiet and good mannered, but she didn't like them. There was something strange about them; they never looked at other customers in the eyes and were very arrogant. Roberta didn't like them either, and one night she asked Luisa where she met them.

"Nowhere," she answered, "they are customers just like any others."

She was always in a hurry to leave at the end of her shift. While waiting for Jose, Natalie looked at her when she drove by in her shinny red car. She sat down thinking she needed a car too, but she didn't have a rich aunt in New York.

The sailor, friend of Luisa, arrived at the restaurant the following Saturday in the afternoon. Natalie was in the kitchen picking up an order. When she came back she saw the sailor give Luisa a packet that she quickly put away in her purse. She smiled at Natalie and tried to explain:

"It is a gift, he always brings me something from his trips, he loves me very much."

Natalie thought it wasn't normal, and didn't answer. The man left in a hurry without waiting for her to end her shift, like most days. The waitresses continued working, but Natalie noticed that Luisa was nervous, looking out the window frequently and spilling the water on the tables.

"You have shaky hands tonight,"

Roberta said, while she smoked her inseparable cigarette behind the counter, when Jose was not there, that is. Luisa didn't answer. She looked out again. It was ten thirty at night. Natalie was very busy serving a customer when she heard Luisa tell Roberta.

"I am going to leave for a moment. I have to talk to somebody on the corner. He is a friend, but he doesn't like it here because, you know, sometimes there are dirty people here and he is a very fine and sophisticated man."

Roberta laughingly commented:

"This girl has a sophisticated friend, and this is no place for them!"

She walked away hastily without answering Roberta, grabbed her purse and went out to the street.

The two women watched her as she walked close to a car parked in front of the restaurant. A man opened the door for her and drove off to the next street, but he wasn't the sailor who she claimed was her boyfriend. Roberta moved her head in a gesture of disapproval. Luisa came back almost at the same time as Jose. She apologized for her tardiness. Roberta looked at her without any comment and told Luis to help Natalie clean the restaurant, now full of dirty papers and cigarette buds.

"We can't count on her any more."

Luis said, while he looked at Luisa. She was putting lipstick on and combing her hair to leave.

"Are you going out again?" he asked her ironically.

"Sure, it is my time to leave, only ten minutes until eleven o'clock"

She said, looking at her watch shining on her wrist. It was an expensive watch, and it awakened Luis' curiosity:

"You know Luisa, I think you must introduce me to your rich aunt in New York, I can will marry her."

He joked.

Natalie's life continued the same. She was working very hard to support her family. She arrived home late and got a few hours of sleep. She wished to work during the day, but that meant dealing with Maria so that was out of the question. Natalie knew she had to find another job, but so far she couldn't find anything better. She felt tired because Luisa didn't help her, and she complained to Irma. She smiled and told her that she was going to talk to her, but she never did. Luisa continued to serve her friends in open defiance of restaurant's rules. They gave her fat tips, but never ordered any food. Finally, Natalie gave up and stopped complaining. She thought that Luisa would leave soon now that she was rich and didn't seem to need this job anymore. Two weeks later, she drove off in her flashy red car with one of her enigmatic friends into the Miami night never to be seen again.

CHAPTER 12

MARIA'S WRATH

AFTER LUISA DISAPPEARED, NATALIE TRIED very hard to find another job. She knew that the restaurant offered very little beyond a subsistence salary. Natalie wanted to find a job that would allow her to be with her children when they came back from school. It was hard for her to leave her children alone.

One Sunday Natalie had to work with Maria because it was Nohemi's day off, and she had no choice. That morning, Rosa went with her mother to the restaurant to help wash the dishes; Luis didn't work on Sundays. Jose had told Natalie that Rosa and Maria could do this job, and he would pay ten dollars for half a day. Natalie didn't like the idea, but the girls convinced her that the work was easy; they only had to wipe off the plates and put them in the dishwasher. Ten dollars was a lot of money for them. They wanted have t-shirts, jeans, rings, and everything other children wore in school. This was a good opportunity to get some of these things their mother couldn't provide. So the girls took turns every Sunday. This Sunday it was Rosa's turn. Jose normally gave them a ride, but he was sick. Natalie and Rosa had to take a bus to go to the restaurant.

The place was full when they arrived. Maria opened earlier than Jose as a way to demonstrate her willingness to be the best. Natalie immediately put on her apron, and started to help Nohemi with the orders, she served coffee and brought the glasses of water. She was too busy to pay a lot of attention to what was happening in the kitchen. But when she went there to pick up an order, she found Rosa crying in a corner of the kitchen surrounded by greasy pots. She was frightened, her face red, her body soaked in sweat.

"What happen dear, are you sick?"

"No," she murmured.

"But Rosa, what happened?"

She still didn't answer, but at that moment, Maria turned towards Natalie:

"I told Rosa not to clean the dishes."

"Why not? Jose authorized my daughters to come in on Sundays to help you. This is the reason I brought Rosa today."

"But he is not here, and I don't need help, she is only going to mess everything up."

"This is not true," Rosa, said, "I do everything right."

"You believe that, but not me."

Natalie was angrier than she had ever been before, and she confronted the woman.

"Listen Maria, you are a very bad person, and God will punish you for making a young girl cry because she wants to work."

"You don't bring God into this." She said.

"Yes I have to say his name because you deserve to be punished."

She laughed very loud and said:

"Wait until Jose comes back and you repeat to him all that you told me now. When he is not here, I am in charge of this restaurant."

She said that as she stepped down from the small stool she used to reach the pans because she was too small. She walked close to Natalie and told her:

"When Jose comes back, I am sure he will put you on the street for insulting me. "Wait." she threatened. "Like my name is Maria, you can be sure you are going to be fired."

But Natalie's indignation was unstoppable, and she understood she couldn't take her insolence anymore. She had suffered long enough, and now she made her 12-year-old daughter cry—that was simply unacceptable.

"Listen witch,"

Natalie said in a strong, challenging voice, stepping forward.

"I am not afraid of Jose or you for that matter. I am leaving immediately and you have to help because the place is full."

Maria changed her attitude suddenly.

"You can't go now."

She said a little worried,

Maria was used to seeing Natalie humiliated in front of her, quiet and somewhat submissive. But this time Natalie was unrecognizable.

"Yes, I am going to leave. Let's go Rosa, this woman is crazy and I can't take her anymore."

"No mami," the girl said. "You are going to be without a job."

"I don't care, I will find another job, where the people are good, not like this horrible woman."

She came back to the counter and closed the register's drawer with a strong hand motion. Maria screamed and cursed inside the kitchen, but Natalie didn't hear her anymore. She took off her apron in a rebellious gesture, threw it on the floor and grabbed her purse.

"I am sorry, but I am leaving. Later I will talk with Jose."

She told Nohemi, who was looking at her in utter disbelief.

"Wait Natalie please," Nohemi said.

But it was too late; Natalie was already out the door.

Natalie and Rosa took the bus back home. They sat down and Rosa asked her mother in a soft voice.

"What are we going to do now, mami?"

She hugged her, trying to hold her tears. She didn't want to make Rosa feel guilty for what happened. She knew they would be in deep trouble if she didn't find another job. Yet, she smiled and told her:

"Don't worry Rosa, today we will talk to Mercedes, our neighbor, and maybe she can help me get a job at the factory she is working at. The other day, they were talking to me about this and they said I might have a chance to get a job because they need machine operators."

"Oh, do you think they can help you?"

"Yes. I am sure, they are very good people."

Natalie was silent and closed her eyes for a moment. The confrontation with Maria just left her drained. She knew this was bound to happen, but not this soon.

CHAPTER 13

THE FACTORY

THE FOLLOWING WEEK NATALIE WAS fortunate enough to find a job. Thanks to her friends, Mercedes and Teresa, she was hired at a plastic bag factory and started immediately. When they learned about Natalie's problem with Maria, they recommended her at the factory where they both worked. Mercedes even offered Natalie a ride to work every day. Natalie's shift started at seven o'clock and finished at four thirty in the afternoon. Natalie felt better because she made a little more money, arrived home early and cooked for her children. She had Saturday and Sunday off, and they could go out sometimes. They returned to a normal family life that for many months seemed impossible.

However, she was worried because the supervisor told her that she had a week to learn the ropes. He was a Latin man in his forties and his name was Eduardo Rodriguez. He had white skin, he wasn't a good-looking man but he was not ugly either. His eyes were small and seem to get smaller when he inspected employees, which he often did.

"Are you the friend of Teresa and Mercedes?"

He asked the first time he saw her.

"Yes, are you Rodriguez"?

"Yes, I am,"

and smiled indifferently, but he observed Natalie's slender body with a lot of interest.

"You will start to work with Ziomara on machine ten this week, after that you will have to do it all by yourself."

He didn't say anything more, and walked towards the machine he was fixing. He was the mechanic and supervisor for twelve women who worked very fast operating the biggest machines Natalie had seen.

She had never worked in a factory before and thus felt intimidated by the size, sound and power of the machines. They looked like iron elephants that produced an incessant deafening sound. They made plastic bags for bread so fast and spewed so many bags that Natalie thought they were magic. On each side of her machine there were two big rolls of plastic. When Ziomara turned it on, the plastic started to extend and fold, while a big hot knife cut and sealed the bag at the same time. After the bags came down the conveyor belt, she put them on small wickets; a counter would tell her many bags were passing through. When it reached 250, she had to put them in a box. Ziomara told Natalie to be very alert; she needed to make sure that exactly 250 bags went to each box because they had to be the exact same weight.

Natalie learned quickly, helping Ziomara first; then doing everything herself. It was a simple mechanical work, and Natalie's fine hands became adept fairly fast. She made sure the 250 bags had the name of the supermarket clear and in correct style and colors. Ziomara sat down close to her, checking her work. Rodriguez, passed by them and asked:

"How is the new girl doing?"

"Very well,"

Ziomara said smiling,

"She doesn't need my help anymore."

The man looked at Natalie, who was closing a box and said,

"That's good because she has to work all by herself on Monday."

Having said this, he turned his back and walked away to another machine.

"He is a little rude" Ziomara said, "but he is not bad."

Natalie smiled, but she didn't make any comment. She didn't know anything about him, and hoped they would get along fine. Ziomara turned out to be a very nice and energetic young woman.

Teresa, Natalie's friend, worked close by and often smiled at Natalie to give her some encouragement. At lunchtime, Teresa would bring her some food because she knew that Natalie was always in a hurry, neglecting herself.

"That's why you are so skinny, because you don't eat enough."

"I am not skinny, besides I don't want to be fat," Natalie would respond with a smile.

"But you have to eat well because otherwise your immune system weakens and you get sick."

Natalie smiled at her, and answered:

"I cannot get sick Teresa. My children need me."

The two friends didn't talk much, only during their ten-minute breaks and at lunchtime. Mercedes was working in another section and Natalie would only see her in the afternoon when she rode home with her. It was her first week at a factory and she felt optimistic.

CHAPTER 14

POEMS UNDER
METALLIC CLAMOR

WHEN NATALIE ARRIVED AT THE factory at seven o'clock the following Monday, Rodriguez told her she had to work on machine three.

"This machine is the easiest and doesn't go that fast. I always put the new operators on this machine."

Natalie followed his orders. Pedro, the young man who worked as Rodriguez' assistant, taught her how to work with the new machine, which was somewhat different from Ziomara's.

"You have to pay attention to the plastic rolls. When you see the roll is going to finish, immediately stop the machine. Otherwise, the roll will run out completely, and it is more difficult to put the new roll on. If you stop the machine on time, we only have to tape it to the new roll, and in five minutes it is ready. Rodriguez doesn't like operators to let the roll run out, be careful please."

"Yes," she replied very seriously. She was ready to work very hard and efficiently, regardless of what she thought of her new job. It was a big windowless warehouse, illuminated only by electric lights, and cooled by noisy fans. Nothing pretty to see, only machines, bags, boxes, and a sea of plastic rolls that were transported from one side to another on forklifts. They were handled by rude men who would seldom say hello to the operators working on the machines. That day was lonely and boring. For a moment she thought about the restaurant; at least she could talk to costumers, some had become her friends. But here she was in "the world of machines," where perpetually moving metal, repetitive noise and heat conspired to make life miserable. Natalie, being sensible and romantic, found it difficult to withstand such conditions. However, she worked well that day. At four thirty in the afternoon, Rodriguez told her that she did everything correctly.

"Thank you." She said, feeling happy about adapting to this new system that she knew nothing about before. She couldn't fail again; or rather she could not allow people to push her around anymore just because she had a different background and education.

After few weeks, Natalie learned to command the machines. She got used to the long days standing up, the never-ending noise in her ears, the loneliness, the heat. She turned the interminable production of bags that fell onto her hands like rainfall into poems. First she thought and then, while the bags were falling, she wrote a little on her notebook, always making sure foreman Rodriguez or forelady Tidra, weren't close to her machine. Tidra was a sweet American lady, but she always kept a vigilant eye on each worker. Natalie knew she had to endure that kind of job, which could not be further from her personality. To beat adversity, she thought of beautiful things; she turned the machines into magic animals and the bags into wonderful rain and snow. Instead of loosing her creative mind to the incredible monotony of eight hours making the same thing, she wrote poems. It was the worst time of her working life for sure, but she managed to produce some of her best writings; all under the metallic clamor of giant machines.

But one day, when Natalie was immersed in her fable, Rodriguez caught her with pen and paper in her hands.

"What are you writing Natalie?"

He startled her, and she looked at him scared. Foreman Rodriguez's small eyes were observing her with a bad curios expression. She covered the paper with her hand and answered smiling:

"It is nothing, sometimes I write words in English, you know I need to learn."

He leaned on the machine that had stopped and continued talking:

"I don't like to interfere with the operators, I let them work freely, but I have noticed that you write a lot, and I don't need writers here, I need good operators. This week the rolls have ran out three times."

After that reprimand from Rodriguez, time passed very slowly for Natalie.

She couldn't write her poems during her time on the machine. It was hard for her; the interminable routine made Natalie immensely bored. The other operators were fine and didn't mind working in the factory making the same thing every day. They were adjusted to this, and Natalie asked herself how they could be there, year after year, making the same thing. She would listen to them talking about their husbands, commenting and criticizing the clothes of coworkers while they were working, but that was not prohibited by Rodriguez. He was stern with her about her writing at work, even though it did not interfere with her work in any way. Sometimes during lunch, she sat down on a plastic roll to write her thoughts on her notebook. This helped her continue enduring her work.

Days and months went by, and pretty soon Natalie found herself working at the factory for one year. Thanks to this job, she had been able to keep her family fed and clothed and living in a nice house. That was important thing for Natalie.

One afternoon, while Natalie waiting for a bus because Mercedes had moved to New York, Natalie had an interesting encounter. She was thinking about buying a car and learning how to drive, but the money she made was not enough for that. The bus was late and she was worried about how she was going to get home. At that moment a car stopped close to her. She saw the driver, and was surprised when Rodriguez opened the window, and said:

"Hello Natalie, do you need a ride?"

"Oh yes, thank you, but I don't know if you go in my direction."

"Where do you live?"

"Well it is a little far from here." She gave him the address.

"It is no problem, I have to pass by that corner on my way home, come in Natalie, I will take you home."

"Thank you Rodriguez, that's very nice of you."

The man opened the door, and Natalie got in the car. They were both silent for a while. She was a little nervous because Rodriguez was never nice to her.

The car went down the same streets the bus took. That day Natalie wore jeans like most people in the factory. After five minutes, she noticed that Rodriguez was looking at her legs. He knew that she was aware of his stare, and smiled.

"You know, Natalie, you have a very beautiful body."

She looked at him astonished; he never said anything like that before.

"Thank you,"

she said in a serious tone and moved her head to look outside.

He noticed that she didn't like his compliment, and continued:

"Are you living alone?"

"No, I am living with my children."

"Oh, I know, you have four children, but any boyfriend or husband maybe?"

"No Rodriguez, why do you ask?"

"Well I would like to invite you to go out one day."

She didn't answer; then he put his hand on Natalie's leg.

She moved a little further away from him and said:

"Don't do that Rodriguez. The fact that you gave me a ride doesn't give the right to take advantage of me. I am a respectable woman."

He took his hand off Natalie's leg.

"I don't want to take advantage, only I want to invite you to go out, I didn't mean anything wrong,"

"Thank you, but I don't want to go out with you because you are a married man."

He smiled ironically, and said,

"You can say that you don't like me, but about being married; no woman pays attention to that anymore. It is about having a good time, a boyfriend etc. My wife doesn't have to know if you go out with me."

She looked at him and answered very seriously.

"Excuse me Rodriguez, but I don't agree. Besides, a relationship between a boss and an employee is never a good one."

"All right, I understand your prejudices."

Natalie didn't answer, and he was silent all the way until they arrived to Natalie's house. She said thank you, but he didn't answer.

"This is going to be a bad thing for me," she thought, "he is going to be more strict with me now."

CHAPTER 15

No Writing Allowed

NATALIE CONTINUED WORKING IN THE plastic-bag factory. Her life stayed the same, except she couldn't write poems anymore. She knew that Rodriguez kept a close eye on her, but he never insisted on his invitation. Natalie was doing a good job, the rolls didn't run off the end again, and she became accustomed to the routine. She was not happy, but her life was somewhat stable. She made friends and sometimes on paydays they would go out to have fan, to drink a glass of wine and to dance at a nearby café or bar they could afford. But she never found any male friend she liked. Natalie thought she was going to stay alone with her children. She had been officially divorced for a few months now, and her friend Teresa insisted she shouldn't continue attached to a marriage that was finished. She understood that, but her heart did not. Love has been elusive thus far.

Another endless and monotonous year went by at the factory. Natalie and her children adapted to the American culture. They celebrated Halloween and Thanksgiving, and learned how to cook turkey with stuffing, sweet potatoes, and pumpkin pie. For Christmas they put up the Christmas tree, and Santa Claus, instead of little Jesus, brought the gifts for Adrian and the girls. The two girls were growing up fast. Rosa was fourteen years old, and becoming a very pretty girl, with long blonde hair, and a slender silhouette. Maria was twelve years old, but she looked older because she was tall, and had an outgoing and joyful personality. Her friends loved her since she was always willing to help in any way. She was pretty too, her dark complexion, long black hair and pretty smile drew a lot of attention. Natalie looked at them in disbelief; it seems impossible they have grown up so fast.

Adrian was nine years old, and that year he had his First Communion. He was very intelligent, loved to play football and spoke English better than Spanish. Everything changes when we live in a different country, Natalie thought. She had changed a little too. She preferred watching television in English, lost her gracious accent from her native city, and became accustomed to living indoors instead of spending a great deal of time outside on the front yard or backyard, as was customary in her tropical hometown. Natalie's life consisted of going to work early in the morning, and coming back home at five o'clock to cook for her children. They had dinner together and later the children did their homework and watched TV sometimes. They went to bed at ten o'clock since they all had to wake up early. Natalie felt happy because her children were growing up good and healthy.

Natalie started to become very popular at the factory. She wrote crossword puzzles during lunch, and she distributed them to her friends to solve them. Some of them were intelligent; although their minds were never too far from the machines they spent so much time with. She knew the destructive power of the machine could have on the mind of its operator. She silently fought the idea of being controlled and manipulated by the mindless machine. Though seemingly adapted and content with her job at the factory, she had decided long before to return to her country rather than continuing working in such a mindless environment for the rest of her life.

Rodriguez was always looking to catch Natalie off guard or doing something inappropriate, but Natalie was a good worker and operator. She was always attentive to her machine, especially checking the rolls that had caused her so many problems before. Pedro had become her friend, and he smiled when he saw her stop the machine on time.

"Natalie, you have changed a lot."

"Yes Pedro, I had to do it."

"Do you like this job?"

No, but I have to do it. I need the money for my children."

"You are always alone. If you want, you can get a man to help you."

The guy looked at her, and knew her reaction.

Natalie smiled. She talked as she continued to tend her machine, checking for imperfections, selecting and discarding defected bags from the endless stream of plastic bags. She stopped talking for a moment while trying to fix the rapidly growing stack of bags. She ten continued when the stack was perfect.

"It is not easy for me Pedro, I have four children, and I have to be careful because I don't want problems in my house. He has to be a special man, and I don't think it is going to be easy to find one like that."

"I am a very special man, didn't you know?"

"Yes, very special," she said smiling, "you have a wife, and several girlfriends that visit you."

"You know Natalie, I am separated from my wife, and the girls that you see are only friends."

"Yes, yes I know."

The young man wiped his forehead; he was sweating profusely in the usual heat of the factory. They both laugh, after all they were only friends, and enjoyed each other's company.

However, even with all the impediments to love, Natalie's heartbeat accelerated without explanation in the presence of a man the following December. It was on the day she went to the factory dressed in a nice red dress and wearing high-heals. She had an appointment with a dentist and needed to be presentable. At lunchtime, when she was walking with Teresa to the place where they sat down to eat their lunch, she saw three men elegantly dressed walking toward them. Teresa identified them:

"The older one is the owner of the factory, the other is the general manager, and the third, I don't know, probably he is a businessman. Sometimes, they bring costumers here to show them the factory."

Natalie looked at them, and noticed they had the personality and self-assurance characteristic of people with money. It is hard not to be self confident when you have money. But she was surprised when she saw the third man. He was a little younger than the other two, had blue eyes and blonde hair. She looked at him, but to her surprise he looked at her too and winked one of his pretty blue eyes. She smiled back, but continued walking. The men walked by the two women and continued to the office on the second floor. She felt her heart palpitating faster in excitement.

"You know Teresa, the man in the blue suit said hello to me, and winked his eye."

"I didn't see anything Natalie, you were probably mistaken, that kind of people never say hello to the operators."

"Why not? We are people too! We support this factory with our work. Isn't that true?"

"Yes, but that's life."

"I don't know why, but one of them looked at me, I swear. Besides, Teresa, you know, that man looks familiar to me. Maybe I have seen him before. I don't know where, but I am sure I have seen him before."

Teresa smiled, and walked quickly to get a table to eat her lunch. Natalie followed her, thinking she would like to see that man again. She felt exited for a while, but by the end of that afternoon her luck changed for the worse.

Natalie had a dictionary in her purse. When the machine stopped and Pedro was changing a roll, she opened it trying to find a word she needed to finish her puzzle. A minute later she felt Rodriguez' presence behind her.

"What are you doing Natalie?" He asked in a cold voice.

She looked at him surprised because she didn't expect him at that moment.

"I am looking for a word in the dictionary."

"I told you, I don't want distractions during work."

"But, Rodriguez, the machine is stopped, Pedro is changing the roll."

"I know, but you don't have the right to read anything during work, you can only do it on your time off."

He was talking slowly, but Natalie noticed in his tone of voice a hidden menace.

She tried to diffuse the situation:

"I am sorry Rodriguez, I didn't know this, I believed when the machine was stopped we could do something else."

"Yes, you can do something else: work! But not that; I told you a long time ago. Now, punch your card and go home. I am going to suspend you for five days."

The bombshell left Natalie without words for a moment. It was very unusual for a supervisor to do that, it never happened to anybody during the time she had been working there. She saw his face, and looked at his small eyes staring at her with fury. Then she answered very nervously.

"You cannot do that; five days without work is too much, you know I have my children."

"You should have thought about that when you didn't obey my orders."

"I didn't do anything wrong, my work is perfect."

"I don't want to discuss it any more, I told you to leave."

"Please Rodriguez, why don't you like me? I have never done anything wrong."

She insisted trying to change his mind but it was useless, the man had decided to send Natalie home.

"Okay, if you won't punch out, I will do it for you."

Walking fast across the factory, he went to the room where the operators punched their cards, looked for Natalie's card and punched it. After that he went toward the office, probably to talk to the boss about the problem with Natalie. She felt an intense humiliation for his rude attitude and injustice. She thought about going to the office and talking with the manager, but later decided it would just be a waste of time. He was a foreman and she was just a simple machine operator. Then she took her thermo of coffee, her purse and without looking at anyone, almost crying, Natalie De La Cruz left the factory at a brisk pace. She looked at her wristwatch. It was two o'clock in the afternoon, at least she could arrive early to the appointment, she thought with resignation. "God knows that I was good, and probably one day, she would find a good man to help me," Natalie thought.

Teresa called her that night. She worried about what happened to her and was upset at Rodriguez, especially how rude and unfair he had been with Natalie. Natalie was clearly affected by it and answered:

"I won't come back, Teresa, it's impossible to put up with him anymore."

"But you can't do this, you need the job, and it is not easy to get another one. Remember you are alone, and you have to take care of your children."

"Yes, I know, but what do I have do? This man hates me, and he wants to fire me."

"But don't let him do that. He is not the owner of the factory. They can change him or remove him anytime and that would be the end of him. I have seen many cases in my five years there. From one day to the next, we would see another supervisor. These things happen but don't let him intimidate you or to keep you from coming back. Come back and pretend nothing happened."

"Do you think so Teresa?" Natalie answered almost crying.

"Yes, I am sure. He can't fire you because you haven't done anything wrong. They have to give you unemployment compensation, and they don't want to do it because it costs them money. Don't worry Natalie, Monday be here at seven o'clock, and act like nothing happened."

Teresa repeated this trying to convince her friend to return to work.

Her friend's voice made Natalie feel better and promised Teresa she would think it over before making a decision. Teresa's words made a lot of sense. Rodriguez was not the owner, and someday things could change. After her conversation with her friend, her daughters noticed Natalie was less worried.

The problem she had with Rodriguez created a lot of anxiety for the whole family. The three girls hugged her with love and told her to listen to Teresa because she had more experience. During her five days at home, Natalie tried very hard to get another job, but she couldn't. Only night shift positions were available in some restaurants she applied to, which would have made it impossible for her to be with her children. She thought that it was her destiny to return to the factory since there was nothing else she could do. That weekend Natalie thought that it would be a good idea for them to take a bus to Disney World, to be a little happy, have some fun with the children. The entire family was saddened by her problem at work, and she decided to change that.

On Saturday morning they took the Greyhound bus to Disney World. The children were very happy and smiling. Natalie felt better and thought it was a good idea to go. She had some savings in the bank and took some money out to spend at Disney for Saturday and come back on Sunday night. They rented a hotel close to Disney World, and spent a wonderful day there. The three girls and Adrian were crazy running around the park looking for the best show. Everything was fun and Natalie felt happy again, forgetting about Rodriguez for a while. As usual, Adrian was looking for toys; he was still a young boy who loved toy cars. But toys in Disney World were too expensive for Natalie, but he always insisted.

"I can't buy that toy, Adrian, I don't have enough money."

Adrian didn't say anything, but in the next minute he was gone. The boy disappeared in the multitudes of people that filled the park every weekend.

"My God, girls" she said, "where is Adrian, I don't see him around"

Eugenia, Rosa and Maria began looking for him, but there were too many people and they came back to Natalie without him.

"We cannot see him either mami, I don't know where he is. It is better if you go to the place where they report missing children." Rosa suggested.

Natalie called the girls and they went to the booth where there was a security guard. She started to explain to the woman about her missing son.

"How old is he?"

"Oh he is eight years old," Natalie answered.

"Tell me what he looks like, fill out this form, and our people will find him soon. Don't worry madam, your son will be here soon."

The woman said with a smile trying to downplay Natalie's fear.

She filled out the paper, explaining what Adrian looked like. She then asked,

"Do we have to wait here?"

"Yes, it is better, sit down in front and wait."

They all sat down anxiously. At that precise moment, a boy appeared from a group of people directly in front of them.

"Mami," Maria said, "I think he is there."

"Where Maria?"

"Over there, he is coming here."

"My God it is him,"

Natalie said and the tears appeared in her eyes. The boy looked at his mom, but he didn't say anything.

"Adrian, my love, where were you?"

Natalie said hugging him.

"You scared the heck out of me! We were so worried looking for you."

"I was there in that corner watching you; remember you didn't buy me the toy."

"That's why you disappeared? You know that it is very dangerous to be alone with so many people."

Maria looked at him and said,

"That was not nice what you did!"

"Yes," added Eugenia, "Your poor mother was crying for you." Don't you ever do that again."

"I am sorry mami," he said, "I won't do that again."

"Okay Adrian, sit here for a moment, I am very tired."

CHAPTER 16

AUGURY

ON SUNDAY NIGHT NATALIE CRIED in her bed before going to sleep because she knew that she had to confront Rodriguez the next day. But on Monday morning the employees at the factory saw a new Natalie walking in. She had a red dress on, very tight, defining her slender body; new high-heels shoes; and her brown hair on her shoulders was stylishly combed. She had makeup on, and her eyes had a very happy and special look.

She walked faster and more graciously than ever, looking for her card, and she punched in at exactly seven o'clock. Her co-workers were astounded to see her so vibrant and optimistic. They started to applaud but quickly realized they may get in trouble with Rodriguez. He was fixing one of the machines and didn't see her at first, but when she passed by his side he heard the sound of high hills. He immediately looked up and saw a pretty woman walking by. He didn't recognize her, but when she sat in her chair and turned her face towards him, he noticed that the woman was Natalie. He was so surprised that he dropped the hammer he was working with. Natalie's friends, especially Teresa, smiled at her, happy to see her so radiant and ready to work again. Natalie had returned, not humiliated, but proud and optimistic, sending a clear message of courage against injustice.

Pedro came to her machine to say hello and told Natalie:

"You are very pretty, everybody was surprised to see you again. I missed you a lot."

"Me too I missed all of you. What do I have to do now?" She asked.

"I don't know. I will ask Rodriguez."

But it wasn't necessary because Rodriguez came to her machine and told Pedro:

"She can work here, but she has to take care of both sides because Sonia wont' be here today."

Sonia was the operator who took care of the other side of Natalie's machine.

"But, Rodriguez," Pedro said, "this machine is faster, I don't know if she can do both sides."

He said trying to help Natalie.

"Both sides, I told you."

And he went back to continue working on the broken machine.

Pedro cursed in Spanish to himself and started both sides of the machine, as Rodriguez demanded.

"It doesn't matter Pedro, I can do it, don't worry."

"Well, if you can't handle the bags, stop the machine. He cannot force you to do both sides."

Natalie smiled, her white teeth contrasted with her lips painted red.

"I can handle this machine. I am going to show Rodriguez what my hands can do."

That morning Natalie worked non-stop until twelve o'clock, except for a ten-minute break. She went from side to side, picking up the bags with incredible speed, taking the bags and putting them in the boxes, like a game. The other operators looked at her with admiration and respect. She was by no means the best operator, but at that moment she demonstrated her abilities. The bell rang to stop the machines and go to lunch. Natalie stopped the machine and went to talk to Teresa. She was happy and puzzled about Natalie's happy return.

"Rodriguez was so surprised when he saw you that he couldn't talk. That was good, I was almost laughing in his face," said Teresa.

"It is better, isn't it Teresa?"

"I am not afraid of him, but he gave the work of two people." Natalie said.

"Yes, he is a bad person, but God is going to punish him, I know."

The two women were walking toward the tables where they usually sat to eat lunch when they saw two elegant men coming towards them. "He is the owner," Teresa said. The man didn't say hello as he passed by them, as was customary for a person in a high position. Natalie watched them too. However, she noticed that the other man looked familiar and smiled at her, which made her feel important. He was the man with blue eyes, blond hair and an agreeable smile. She felt a strange sensation in her body and suddenly remembered him. She had seen him before at the restaurant she used to work at. She smiled back nervously. Was he really smiling with her? Who was this man so different from the rest in this hellish factory?

"Teresa, did you see the other man? He said hello to me, I think it is the same man I saw the other day. I told you about him. I hoped that he would come back, he is marvelous."

Teresa smiled at the thought of Natalie showing interest in a man for the first time.

"You know Natalie I didn't pay attention to them, I was checking my lunch. I think it is enough for both of us. I am sure you didn't bring anything."

"Thank you Teresa," she said. But Natalie had lost her appetite. The smile of this man had made her very emotional, and she didn't know why. When they first talked at the restaurant, he told her he came to Miami on business; something related to plastic bags. Miami was a big city and to stumble upon the same man in two very different places, and under different circumstances was almost impossible. Was this a highly unusual coincidence or an augury? Natalie put on her usual illusion-proof armor and thought she will never see him again. By now she was accustomed to the adversities that seemed to be reserved for poor immigrants working in factories or restaurants.

"I'm sure I won't see him again in my life."

She concluded as she returned to her machine to tackle the work of two people.

CHARTER 17

SCOTT

JANUARY BROUGHT SEVERAL DAYS OF intense cold, which was particularly hard for Natalie. Every morning she had to walk two blocks to take the bus at the corner, wearing a heavy coat. It was still dark when she got to the bus stop and she had to stay under the light post to make sure the bus driver would see her. Even though the driver knew her, she couldn't take any chances. Arriving late at work was not an option since Rodriguez was clearly looking for an excuse to fire her. It was here under the dim street light, on a cold Miami morning that Natalie promised to herself she would return to her country unless her working conditions improve soon. She would rather go back and face defeat than continuing living in a foreign country without work rights, and living on the verge of poverty. Her lack of work permit was keeping her subdued to a job she hated and a supervisor who seemed to have the authority to fire her anytime for any reason.

Her relation with Rodriguez continued to be tense. He only talked to her when it was absolutely necessary, kept a watchful eye on her and demanded more productivity. Natalie didn't dare take another book to her machine. Only during lunchtime was she able to read or write anything. She had to be extra careful because of his constant vigilance. Yet, she didn't feel defeated; something inside kept telling her to wait. She was not exactly sure what for.

Then she saw that man with the blue eyes again. He was looking at a machine with another man from the office. Natalie thought that he was probably a new mechanic. She was happy because he seemed like a pleasant person different from all the others she had met in the factory. She saw them from a distant, and they disappeared into the office later. She wished he would look at her again, but that was probably an illusion.

She commented that to Teresa and she laughed.

"Don't get excited, Natalie, you don't know if he is only a visitor, and you probably won't see him again."

"He could be a mechanic, they need a lot of them here." Natalie added.

"I don't know, but he doesn't look like a mechanic."

Teresa said, and this time she saw him up close. Then Natalie felt sad. She was thirty-five years old and her heart still longed for love. She didn't have much luck with the two men she had loved. Her ex-husband and another man, both failed to understand her. The words of Teresa echoed in her mind, and she quickly lost hope for this man whose name she didn't even remember. However, she continued looking towards the office. She knew he had to come out again.

At that point her machine started malfunctioning; the big cutter was not working properly and bags began falling. Rodriguez came and told her he had to change the cutter. He sent Natalie to another machine. As she was walking, she looked towards the office again and saw the man with the blue eyes. She froze without thinking, and watched him for a moment. He was walking fast towards her, and as he got closer she recognized him. It was Scott Johnson; the name came back to her instinctively. The man she met at the restaurant several months earlier, there was no doubt now. He smiled.

"How are you?" It's great to see you again Natalie. How are your children?

"Very well, thank you," she answered with emotion.

His blue eyes were gleaming with excitement. She looked deep into his eyes and saw the brightness that suddenly seemed to light up the entire dark factory. She continued on to her machine, and he went out. She got very emotional as she realized that he wasn't a customer or a visitor, but most likely an employee of the same factory. She wished this was not a dream. She was hopeful he would come back to see her because he was working there too.

However, a week passed and Natalie didn't see Scott again. She wanted to know for sure if he was working in the factory, but none of the operators knew anything about him. Not even Pedro, who seemed to know everything and everybody in the factory, knew. He answered her questions with an indifferent gesture:

"I don't know who that American guy is. Why are you interested in him?"

"No, no, I am just curious."

"Well, you better take care of your machine."

"I do that very well."

Natalie said a little disappointed.

Pedro was serious; he looked as though he was jealous of Natalie's interest in the American guy.

Then something totally unpredictable happened. Natalie will never forget that morning thereafter when she arrived at seven o'clock and found a group of workers gathering around the main office. Teresa, who was among them, called her and said in a soft voice:

"Have you heard the news?"

"What news, Teresa?"

She whispered:

"You know, they are going to change Rodriguez, he wont' be foreman anymore. He was demoted to a mechanic. A new foreman was hired to replace him, he is an American."

"It can't be possible." Natalie said.

"Tidra, told me. Today, at lunchtime they will come here to introduce him to us.

"Who is he?" Natalie asked.

"We don't know, Tidra said, she knows him and he is terrible."

"Why did she say that?"

"Because he is very strict, and doesn't allow anybody to be late to work."

Natalie smiled and replied:

"It doesn't matter who he is, he can't be worse than Rodriguez, for me."

"The other operators are scared, you know that many of them did whatever they wanted, and he never said anything."

"It is true, they are his friends; now everything is going to change."

There was a sense of excitement and anticipation among the workers in the factory. A new foreman was coming, and they didn't know anything about him. Even though Rodriguez had a bad temper and a caustic personality, most machinists were used to him and they understood each other. A new foreman may mean new rules, more work or trouble for some of them. A sort of collective nervousness was palpable among the women that morning as they were getting ready to start the workday. One of them, Yolanda, told Natalie as she walked by her:

"You must be happy, but you never know, you may be the first to be fired by the new man."

Natalie ignored her. Certainly, she was happy and hoped that the new foreman wouldn't be as bad as Rodriguez. Nothing will be worse than Rodriguez who picked on her for no apparent reason. He was working on a broken machine and giving orders like nothing happened. But Natalie noticed an undeniable indignation on his face.

After lunch, Tidra, called the operators for a meeting and announced that people from the office were going to talk to all the workers.

"Then it is true." Natalie thought.

She was close to Teresa, waiting anxiously for the new supervisor. After few minutes, three men came out of the office and stopped in front of the waiting crowd. Natalie tried to see who they were but she was only able to recognize Mr. Caswell, the general manager. Because of the many people in front of her, she was not able to see the other two.

Finally she found a gap in the crowd saw them. One was an American man, who was addressing the workers in Spanish. The other—to her absolute astonishment—was Scott Johnson, the man who miraculously crossed her path twice in very different circumstances. At that moment she didn't know which one of them was the new foreman. She expected to be the man speaking in Spanish to the crowd. Then he finally introduced the new foreman: Scott Johnson!

Natalie could not believe it. His friend, the American guy with blue eyes as calm as a lake, was her new supervisor.

"God, it is impossible, I can't believe it! It is a dream, and very soon I would wake up and find Rodriguez again behind me, telling me that the roll was gone."

But it was not a dream. He started to talk in English with a clear and serious voice that she was able to understand well. He said that he will try to be a good boss for them, and he expected the cooperation of all the operators to improve production and efficiency because the company was going through difficult times. He also said that he would interview every operator to listen to her or his problems. People applauded loudly, and Scott smiled happily and gratefully. Natalie couldn't take her eyes off him.

She admired him, and she knew that he would be a good boss. His clear blue eyes would not lie, she was sure.

When he finished talking, the operators returned to their machines to continue working. They were making comments, some of them were disappointed, others were indifferent, few were happy. Rodriguez talked to some of his favorites, and he made a disdainful gesture, looking toward the office. Then he returned to his job, fixing the machines as he had been doing for many years. Natalie saw him and thought:

"He was always a mechanic, and he will always be a mechanic. He didn't understand how to deal with people."

Natalie came back to her place, silent but happy. She felt like a little caged-bird whose door had just been opened. Scott went to his office with the other men. She watched him as he walked up the stairs. He was agile and had a slender and strong body. He wasn't too tall, but very attractive. She sighed, and wondered if he would look at her again. Now he was her boss, possibly everything would be different. There was a lot of distance between them. But she couldn't forget the way Scott looked at her, with admiration, like she was someone special to him. Maybe her luck was about to change.

CHAPTER 18

UNEXPECTED VISIT

LIFE CERTAINLY CHANGED FOR NATALIE since Scott started as the new supervisor. He was different from Rodriguez in every way. He looked closely at the production of every operator and when expectations were met, he congratulated them with a smile. Scott interviewed each of them in his office. Because many workers did not speak English, he used an assistant to translate to Spanish.

Natalie was very nervous when it was her turn for her interview, but Scott smiled at her and she felt better. He asked many questions in English that Natalie understood fairly well, but his assistant repeated everything in Spanish anyway. He asked her if the company had ever increased her salary.

"No, never, I have to buy my clothes at the flea market."

Both men laughed. Scott watched her with a sweet look. Then he wrote something on his notebook and told her:

"Natalie, we will give you $.50 cents more per hour, starting next week."

"Oh thank you, I would appreciate that."

"You deserve it, your production is very good and I hope you don't have to buy your clothes in the flea market anymore."

They smiled again and Natalie felt very emotional. This was the first they talked about money in the factory. He increased the salary of every operator and, as a result, he became very popular. Employees changed their bad attitude toward him. After that production increased.

One day at lunchtime, while Natalie was reading a book sitting on a roll of plastic, Scott walked by her and said:

"Hello Natalie, do you like to read?

"Yes, I like to read very much, but only during my lunch."

She answered afraid he would know about her problem with Rodriguez regarding her reading and writing at work.

"I like that you read, there is nothing wrong with that. I noticed you are reading a book in English."

"Yes, I can read better than I speak."

She said, trying to pronounce the words well.

"No, you speak good, I can understand everything."

"Thank you Scott, but English is not easy."

"No, it is not easy, but Spanish is difficult too for me."

They both smiled and he looked at her again with a sweet look.

For a moment they were silent, and then Scott said something that surprised her.

"Excuse me Natalie, do you mind if I ask a question?

But he didn't wait for the answer.

Are you married?"

"No, I am divorced and I have four children, three daughters and one son."

"I have two sons."

She didn't continue with the conversation. Her limited English and her emotions got on her way. At that moment she couldn't understand the extent of his question, but she noticed some interest in his eyes. Scott talked some more about productivity and before leaving he asked her:

"Listen Natalie, I would like to move close to the factory. I live too far from here. Do you happen to know where I can rent an apartment around here?

"Oh yes," she said, "there is a good house close to me for rent. It could be good for you."

"Well, tomorrow is Saturday, do you have time to go with me to show me the house?"

"Yes I can, I don't have any plans for tomorrow."

Can you give me your phone number? I will call you at nine in the morning if you don't mind. I don't know your address."

Natalie looked at him, feeling very happy. She gave him her phone number and he wrote it on his small address book.

"Okay Natalie I will see you tomorrow. Thank you."

He turned around and started to walk toward his office. Natalie watched him until he disappeared inside. Her hands were cold and she felt a little hope in her heart.

He was going to visit her. He told her he would call at nine in the morning. Next morning she woke up at seven so she would have time to fix the house and have everything clean when he arrived. She made coffee and went out to see the tree in the garden. She enjoyed the fresh morning air. It was a pleasant day of perfect temperature and she went outside without a sweater. The sun started to come out from behind the clouds and one ray of light illuminated the horizon. She was contemplating that with admiration when she had a premonition: her life was going to change for the better and she would not have to return to her country defeated and penniless. There were going to be dark clouds in her life, but the sun would always send a shinning ray to illuminate her life. Everything around her looked beautiful that morning and full of life. The little birds in the tree were singing and Natalie listened, enchanted. The promise to see Scott made her feel different, and she noticed that nature was incredibly pretty. But she cautioned herself. It was too early to expect anything from Scott. It may all be a vane illusion.

When the children woke up at eight o'clock they found her cleaning and vacuuming the house.

"Mami, why did you wake up so early?" Maria asked her. "Remember today is Saturday."

Natalie smiled.

"I know it is Saturday, but it is possible that my boss will come to visit us this morning. He wants to find a house close to his job."

"The man that suspended you for five days? I don't want to see him around here."

"No, he is not the one. That was Rodriguez and he is not my boss anymore. Now I have a new boss, his name is Scott and he is a very good person."

Rosa came from the kitchen with a cup of coffee and asked her mother:

"Is he handsome?"

Natalie smiled:

"Why do you say that?"

"You are very happy, I haven't seen you like this in a long time."

Natalie tried to dodge her question: "No he is not; he is only a good boss, and he doesn't make my life miserable like the other one did."

"Oh that's good. At what time is Scott coming here?"

"First he will call me, he said at nine o'clock, and I am waiting for his call."

"Does he speak Spanish mom?" Maria asked.

"No, he is an American."

"Then, how do you talk to him?" she said smiling.

"You don't think that I can speak English? I understood everything he said, and he understood me too."

"I am teasing you, I know you speak English."

"Not like I wish I could," Natalie said. "I know I have to study English, but I can't do it now."

Natalie knew Maria was right. She didn't speak English well enough, and Scott had to repeat himself often when they were talking.

At nine o'clock the phone rang, and sure enough it was Scott on the other end. He said hello and announced he would be there at ten thirty. He sounded happy and Natalie felt good listening to him. She repeated the address of her house. He is going to visit her, and she would have the opportunity to talk longer without her coworkers gossiping and criticizing. She knew that he wouldn't say anything special, but at the least he would sit down for a while to talk, and he would have a chance to meet her children.

Scott was punctual. He parked his late model car in front of the house. The children looked out the window to see him. Adrian abandoned the crossword puzzle he was doing on the table and ran to see his mother's boss. Scott opened the car door, checked the paper with the address and walked towards the front door. Scott was wearing shorts, a sports t-shirt and athletic shoes. He looked forty in the factory but now he appeared younger and happier. Natalie asked the children to move way from the window and wait for Scott to come in. He knocked on the door and Natalie opened it. She was wearing jeans and a pink blouse that went well her light complexion. She had light make up on, and her hair was combed neatly. She looked pretty and young. Scott was clearly impressed by her radiant morning look. He had never seen her dressed like that.

"Come in, please and sit down."

"Thank you Natalie, your house is pretty and it is in a good location."

"Thank you, but please sit down, would you like a cup of coffee? I always make American coffee."

"Thank you Natalie, but I don't want to bother you, I had one before I left home."

"But that was one hour ago. I am going to bring it in a moment."

When Natalie went to the kitchen, Scott looked at her pretty body and noticed the tight jeans she was wearing. While he was drinking his coffee, Natalie called her children to meet him. The girls walked in the living room, said hello and introduced themselves in correct English. Scott talked to them for a while and told Natalie they were very pretty. Later, Adrian came to say hello too. Scott talked to him about school and other things, but Adrian was shy and spoke little. But when Scott mentioned football, he immediately changed and started a lively conversation.

Natalie was observing him, and she noticed that he was a cultured man who knew how to treat children. Her daughters were pretty, but he didn't stare at them as other men did. Scott's eyes had an honest look, and she knew he would never do anything wrong to her daughters. One way Natalie gauged men was by how they look at her daughters. She knew how dangerous an ill-intentioned man could be to her daughters. It was true that Scott only looked at her. Natalie didn't know if there would ever be anything serious between them, but Scott had passed the first test, and the most important one for her. She would prefer to be alone than putting her children at risk.

After a while the girls excused themselves and went to watch television in their bedroom. Adrian went to the yard to play with his football. Natalie, and Scott were alone in the living room.

"Natalie your children are very nice and well educated," he said.

"Thank you, I am glad that you think so"

"Yes, I am sure. It is very difficult to educate children now because the parents are very busy working. I have two children, five and three years old. Next Saturday I will bring them if you would like to meet them. They are staying with their mother."

She felt his blue eyes looking at her intensely. Natalie thought at that time that he wanted to continue with their friendship.

"Oh, I would love to see them, they can play with Adrian in the yard."

Yes, I think so. They could be good friends. My children love to play baseball, football, and they love the beach. I would like to take them to the beach next Sunday. Would you like to go, Natalie?"

He asked her out of the blue.

"Yes Scott, I would like that very much."

They looked into each other's eyes smiling. Then he remembered why he came and asked Natalie to go with him to see the house for rent. Natalie called Eugenia and Rosa and explained that they were going to see a house for Scott. She asked them to take care of Maria and Adrian.

"Okay mami, don't worry." Rosa said.

They went out and Scott opened the car door for Natalie, and she felt appreciated. Her children looked at them through the window and she noticed that Rosa and Maria were smiling. Apparently Scott had passed the test with them too. They have never smiled at any other admirers who came to the house before. They went to see the house for rent, but nobody was there. There was only a phone number written on a piece of paper and taped to the door, and Scott wrote it in his notebook. Later they went to see another apartment for rent, but Scott didn't decide on anything. She had the impression that he was looking for something better.

In the afternoon, he invited her to the park that was close to her house. She had been there with her children sometimes. The park was big and covered by thick, green foliage and large oak trees that protected them from the sun. They sat on a bench and started to talk like good old friends. He told her something about his life, his children, marriage and divorce.

"It was just an attraction, and not love. We really never loved each other."

He didn't say anything more and Natalie didn't ask either. She listened to him but she was very discreet. She also told him a little about her life. He interrupted her and asked if she had a boyfriend. At that moment he looked at her very close, and Natalie started to feel a mutual attraction. She changed her look and answered.

"No Scott, I don't have a boyfriend."

He smiled and said:

"That's strange because you are very beautiful."

"Thank you Scott, but I don't think so. Don't forget my children."

"That has nothing to do with it, your children are very good."

"Yes, but it is not easy to find somebody capable to loving me and them too.

That's part of the reason I am alone."

"It is not fair, Natalie, you have to think of yourself too."

She didn't answer because it was too difficult to explain to him her problems in English. She just smiled at him. He took her hand for the first time and caressed it. She sighed without moving her hand and was overcome by emotion. His hand was warm and soft. They were silent for a long time, looking at the trees that were moving with the afternoon breeze.

"I like the trees,"

Natalie managed to say, excited like a young girl in her first date. He could have hugged and kissed her because they were alone, and the passion was mutual. Yet, he didn't try to. At the end of their wonderful day he kissed her on the cheek as they said goodbye at the front door of her house.

CHAPTER 19

AN INVITATION

THE FOLLOWING WEEK WASN'T VERY happy for Natalie because Scott treated her like usual, nice and considerate, but distant, without mentioning anything about his visit to her house. He would walk by her machine, looked at her and said hello with a smile, but avoided any intimacy. She noticed he looked worried and, according to Pedro, he was working very hard often staying late at the factory. Production was down that week and the bosses were demanding more. There were two machines down and Rodriguez was very slow to fix them. Rodriguez didn't forget that Scott replaced him. He was now trying to belittle and hurt him by delaying fixing the machines.

On Friday when Natalie walked toward the small dinning room to eat her lunch, Scott bumped into her. He stopped to talk to her, but he didn't have pleasant smile.

"How are you Natalie?"

"Very well, and you?" she answered.

"Okay, this Saturday I have to work. There are many problems to solve and it is necessary to complete a large order. Monday is going to be a very hard day and it is possible we may have to work overtime. I have to talk to the operators."

"Oh, I see."

She replied looking into his eyes. She noticed he was very worried. She understood that the plans he mentioned last week were cancelled. He probably forgot what he said about visiting her with his children. He didn't say anything else except for a cold "I will see you later," which sounded more like a breakup to her.

When Natalie returned to her machine after lunch, her new helper on the machine, Sonia, told her something that troubled her greatly.

"You know Natalie, on Saturday I saw you with Scott in his car and you looked very happy. You are very fast. I am surprised."

"In what sense am I fast? You mean working on the machine?"

She was silent for a moment, then continued telling Natalie:

"You are fast, not only on the machine, but in handling men you are better."

Natalie was stunned. She looked at her and saw a very serious look on her face. Her black eyes had an evil expression. Women didn't joke about that. Then Natalie answered in the same tone.

"I don't know what you are talking about, but if you are referring to Scott and I, listen to this. I don't have to give you any explanation about my life, but I have to do it because I don't want to hear any rumors. There is nothing between us; we are only friends. I was with him because he wants to rent an apartment close to my house. Please don't repeat that because he is a very good boss, and he doesn't deserve those rumors."

She was silent and picked up the bags quickly. Later, she smiled with a certain sneer and told Natalie something that perturbed her.

"Anyway, Scott is impossible for us. I have been calling him at the phone number he gave me, and a woman always answers. I don't know who it is, but I think she is his wife."

"He told me, that he was divorced." Natalie replied.

"Men always say many things, but most of the time they are lies."

"I don't think he is a liar," Natalie countered, somewhat disappointed. "As a matter of fact, why do you call him so frequently? I never call him, but I prefer not to talk about this anymore."

But Sonia insisted.

"He gave me his phone number because he wants to get an apartment closer to work. The same thing he did with you. You don't believe that? Who is the woman that answers the phone, and always says he is not at home? To me, he is a liar. I will never call him again. I don't like to waste my time, and I don't care if you want to go out with him."

Natalie didn't answer her and quietly went about her work, now faster than before. Sonia noticed Natalie's unwillingness to continue with the conversation, made a disapproval gesture and concentrated on her work too.

Natalie felt tormented. No matter how hard she tried to avoid this sentiment, Sonia had succeeded in sowing the seed of doubt in her mind.

She didn't know if Sonia was telling the truth, or if she was envious because she liked Scott. In any case, this uncertainty kept her mortified all afternoon. Finally, at four o'clock she left to take the bus, always thinking about the same thing. During the trip to her house she remembered the time she spent with Scott in the park, and she thought it was impossible that he was a liar. His eyes had a clear and sincere look. There had to be another explanation. Natalie would like to ask him, but she wouldn't. She didn't have the right to ask such a question, besides he may not visit her again if she did. Moreover, she was an operator and he was the boss. It would not look very professional for a supervisor to be involved in relationship with an employee, especially of lower rank. Those rumors spread by workers like Sonia could be harmful to Scott, who had just started in that position. That may be the real reason for Scott's distant attitude toward Natalie throughout the week. Natalie consoled herself with that thought. He was backing off to protect his job and reputation. What he showed the previous Saturday was pure and real. She knew there was an attraction between them, but she couldn't be sure about Scott. She simply had to wait.

The factory became again a place of darkness and depression for Natalie. She couldn't see the sun or the trees that now had yellow leaves. She could only see the high walls that looked like a jail, and the electric lights illuminating the machines. The word "production" seemed to be the only thing that had any meaning. That week the operators were working very hard, and all of them helped Scott complete the order they needed. Natalie was working very hard too, closing her mind to thoughts that led to love. Finally they finished their job and the boxes were closed and sent out on the company trucks.

Scott summoned the employees and with a smile he said,

"Thanks to all of you; I appreciate your effort to help us complete the order."

He said the same to Natalie, but nothing more. To him she was just another operator, she thought, and she tried to conform to this situation. It wasn't easy because she had high hopes about their friendship. She tried to think of other things, to share more with her friends. On Friday, she accepted an invitation by Pedro to go out with other coworkers, including Sonia, for some drinks and maybe dancing. Natalie decided to go with them because she needed to clear her mind and think about other things.

That place was packed with happy people, some dancing to the tune of Latin music. A friend invited Sonia to dance, and Natalie stayed at the table talking to Pedro. She wasn't used to drinking wine, and after the first glass she was happy and excited about the music. Pedro invited her to dance his favorite song "Pedro Navaja" the new salsa hit that had just begun to play. Pedro was from Puerto Rico, and quickly demonstrated his ability as a dancer. They had a good time until nine o'clock, when Natalie decided to go home because she had to take care of her children.

Sonia and Natalie didn't talk about Scott anymore and were friends again. But it was never the same; something had come between them. However, Sonia was very different from Natalie and very soon she lost interest in Scott. Instead, she turned her attention to another man who had started to work in the Extrusion Department, where plastic was made. Natalie clung to the idea of Scott.

Days went by and Scott's attitude changed little. Inell and Thomas, a nice couple that had been working in the factory for a long time, were going to retire that week. Tidra planned a farewell party for lunchtime. All the operators agreed to bring something for Inell and Thomas's party, including Natalie, who wasn't a good cook and paid Irma to bring chicken with rice from her restaurant.

The night before the surprise-lunch for Inell and Thomas in the factory, Natalie received a good surprise herself: Scott called her. When she heard his voice on the phone, her hands turned cold and her voice barely coherent.

"Natalie," he said, "can you hear me?"

"Yes, I am okay, and you?"

"Very good, I am sorry I couldn't go to your house last week, but you know it was impossible, the problem with production, the machines and many other things."

"I know; don't worry Scott, thank you for calling me."

"Listen Natalie, do you know about the party for Inell and Thomas?"

"Oh yes, we are going to have a special lunch for them tomorrow."

"I see, but they are going to have another party on Saturday at their daughter's house. They are going to have a very good party that evening. Do you have an invitation? I received one today."

"No, I don't have an invitation yet, probably she will give it to me tomorrow."

"I hope that you can go Natalie. Everybody from the office will be there on Saturday, you call me when you receive the invitation?"

"Sure, I would like to go, I will tell you tomorrow, but I don't have your phone number."

He was a little surprised.

"You don't have my phone Natalie?"

"No, you never gave it to me."

"Oh, I almost went crazy with the problems at the factory, there is too much work there."

Natalie finally got Scott's phone number. They talked for a while, and Natalie was so happy. But she worried because she didn't know if Inell would invite her to that party. Scott called her because he probably wanted to go with her to the party.

"God! How can I get that invitation for the party?"

She had to find a solution, it was her only chance to be with him; otherwise he would invite someone else. She thought.

Teresa had been talking that day about the special party on Saturday, but she warned that,

"this party is only for the people in the office; Tidra told me that none of the operators were invited to this party, and that we had to be satisfied with the lunch party."

Natalie was very impressed when she thought about Scott's words. He didn't differentiate between people in the factory. The operators in the plant weren't considered the same as the people working in the office, Teresa told her, and now she understood.

"No operators were invited to the special party."

Does that mean she couldn't go with Scott on Saturday night?

"No, but I have to find a way to get an invitation."

That night Natalie sat at her table silently. She asked herself: "What thing do you know how to do?" Something in her mind answered, "You know how to write! Yes, I know how to write" . . . . What are you waiting for? Write Natalie, write!"

She took the pen and wrote a poem to Inell and Thomas about their last day in the factory. But it was in Spanish and she couldn't make a good translation in English. Another idea came to Natalie's mind.

"Rosa, come here please," she called.

"What happened mother, you look like you are on another planet."

The girl came close to her mother and was watching her with interest.

"What did Scott tell you that you are acting so different?"

"It is a problem I have Rosa, I need an invitation to go with him to a party."

And she explained to her daughter her predicament.

"Well, what do you want me to do?

"You can translate the poem Rosa. I just wrote a poem for those people, and I think Inell will invite me when she reads it. You know American people like poems a lot, they would appreciate that, I am sure."

"Okay mami, you can get this invitation, it is not a problem."

"Yes Rosa, it is a big problem, I wrote the poem in Spanish, and I want you to translate it into English."

Rosa looked at her like she was crazy, and she moved her head negatively.

"No mami, you know that I can't do that."

"Yes you have to do it for me, you know English well."

"But a poem is different, I can never translate that; your ideas are very high and I don't think like you."

"No Rosa, it is not a difficult poem, it is simple, read it and you will see that you can do it. Besides I will show it to Scott tomorrow so he can correct it if something is not properly translated."

"When do I have to make that translation, mami?"

"Right now. Tomorrow I have to give it to her to get the invitation for that party."

"I can't, it is ten o'clock."

"Please Rosa, you have to help me."

Natalie kissed her, and the girl took the paper her mother wrote and sat at the table. She started to translate, looking through a big dictionary. At twelve o'clock she called her mother to tell her she had finished.

"I knew you could do it," Natalie said.

"But you better show it to Scott for correction. You know that I am not an expert."

"Yes dear, I appreciate it a lot."

Natalie kissed Rosa with love, and she went to bed thinking that her idea would have a good result.

The next morning when Scott passed close to Natalie's machine, she called him to show him the poem she had written for Inell and Thomas. He took the paper and read it with interest.

"This is very good, Natalie, I am impressed. You have a poetic mind."

"Thank you Scott, but I would like to ask you if you could correct it since I wrote it in Spanish and my daughter Rosa translated it. She thought it might need correction. You know, some Spanish words are not easy to translate into English."

"Yes, I understand. I am going to my office and I will read it more carefully. I will return it to you in a while."

He walked toward his office and Natalie anxiously waited. It was ten o'clock and the lunch party was going to be at twelve.

It was eleven thirty when Scott came back. He approached her machine and returned the paper with some corrections.

"Thank you Scott, but still I would like a favor, can you read this for them at lunchtime? The pronunciation is difficult for me."

"It is not true, you speak very well. You have a different accent, but it is natural. However, if you want I will read it."

"I would appreciate it if you could read it. I will do it in Spanish, but now I need to write the poem on this beautiful card I bought."

"Very good, I will see you at twelve o'clock."

That morning Sonia was sick, and Natalie felt a little better without her presence, always checking her movements. Scott went to a machine that needed his attention and Natalie started to write the poem on the card. She was done in ten minutes. She then showed it to Tidra who passed by her machine. She read the poem, and smiled looking at Natalie with admiration.

"It is a very good poem, I will tell Inell that you wrote it for them."

The party started at twelve o'clock, and all the operators and workers in the other departments gathered around the big tables Tidra and others had prepared for the occasion. There was plenty of delicious food to satisfy everyone. Scott came down before lunch and announced that Natalie had written a poem for a "nice couple" and she wanted him to read it for them. People quieted down and Scott's voice sounded clear and strong so that everybody could hear. People who understood English were surprised by the words Natalie had written. Inell and Thomas listened very intently and when he talked about the sadness for their absence and separation, Inell sobbed, and Thomas smiled with certain sadness. No doubt, the poem had touched them deeply. The couple hugged Natalie who was very nervous by the prospect of reciting it in Spanish in front of everybody. She did it in her peculiar soft voice. Everybody applauded and congratulated her. She had written a very beautiful poem, and people had been moved by it. It was a triumph! Only Rodriguez was silent, perhaps thinking that Natalie was more intelligent than he thought.

"I know what she wants, and it is possible she can get it"

At one o'clock the operators returned to work on their machines. Scott went to his office. Teresa smiled at Natalie and said,

"Beautiful poem you wrote. I would like you to write one for me."

"Some day, you are my best friend."

However happy and appreciated Natalie felt, her wish had not been realized yet. At three o'clock, when she was busy working, Tidra came and handed her a "little invitation card," as she put it.

"Thank you, I appreciate that"

Natalie responded, trying to hide her excitement. But nobody knew how happy she really was.

"Don't say anything to anyone else," Tidra said, "there are so many, and Inell said it is impossible to invite all of them."

That night Natalie waited for Scott to call, but he didn't. Maybe he was waiting for her call too. Then she called the number he had given her. Scott answered immediately,

"Hello Natalie, I was waiting for your call."

"How are you Scott, did you say you were waiting for my call?"

"Yes Natalie, I told you that, remember?"

"Oh yes, thank you for everything you did at the party. Inell liked what I wrote."

"But it was not for me you wrote the poem. You are very good Natalie."

"Thank you again,"

"Listen Natalie, do you have your invitation?"

"Yes I do."

"Then are you going to the party on Saturday?" Scott asked,

"I don't know, none of my friends are invited."

"But you have a friend that is going."

"Who?" Natalie asked,

"Me."

CHAPTER 20

LOVE

THE FOLLOWING AFTERNOON NATALIE STARTED to get dressed early because she knew Scott was very punctual and she did not want to make him wait. He said at six o'clock. She wanted to look elegant and different from the factory operator Scott was used to seeing. She put on a pretty blue silk dress that defined her slender body perfectly. The dress had a slit on the side. Irma, Rosa and Maria helped her put on make up, and combed her hair in the latest style. She wore high-heal shoes in black. When Natalie looked in the mirror, she saw a sophisticated and elegant lady. She smiled and though Scott would probably admire her that night.

"Mami" Maria, said, "You look beautiful in blue."

"Yes," added Rosa. "You will be the best at the party."

"Thanks my dears, I hope it will be true."

"What time are you going to come back, mami?

Adrian asked as though he was worried because his mother was leaving for the party. She hugged and kissed him.

"Very soon Adrian, probably, at ten o'clock. It is only a dinner. Be good with your sisters, and eat your food, and go to bed early."

One minute after six, a car stopped at Natalie's house. The girls ran to window:

"Mami you would die." Said Rosa.

"Why should I? Natalie said, "Is it Scott?"

She was still in front of the mirror in her room.

"Yes he is here and very handsome, in a dark blue suite, a red tie, everything perfect."

"He is coming mami, take your purse, and don't forget the key. We will be sleeping when you come back." Maria said.

Scott was at the door dressed impeccably. Maria opened the door. He entered the house, and said hello to the girls politely. The girls liked him and they were happy that their mother was going to the party with him. He didn't sit down.

"I don't know how to get to this address, I might have to spend some time looking for it. Is your mother ready?"

"I am here,"

Natalie said, walking into the living room.

"How are you Scott, you are very elegant."

"Thank you," he said, and shaking her hand softly. "You are very beautiful."

He looked at her with admiration and a bit surprised; he had never seen her in a cocktail dress. Natalie kissed her children and left with Scott. He opened the car door for her like the first time. Natalie felt happy as she waved goodbye to her children looking out the window. She sensed that this night was going to be very important for her. Scott was looking at her and she noticed that he liked her legs that looked pretty in her nylon stockings.

During the trip Scott told her about his aspirations to open up a business with a friend. Natalie didn't talk much, but listened carefully. She felt so happy to go with him that she didn't find many English words to express herself. They arrived a little late to the dinner party after getting lost looking for the address. As they walked into the house, they noticed everybody staring at them. Apparently, they were not expecting Scott to be with an operator from the factory. However, they welcomed them cheerfully, and Inel's daughter took a picture of them. Natalie looked unusually radiant, impressing everybody with her elegance and good manners.

Scott felt very proud to have her by his side and he didn't miss an opportunity to please her. They sat down at a table with other people. He drank whisky; she preferred fruit punch with liquor. After a while they served a buffet that included a variety meats, vegetables, rice, potatoes, fruits and deserts. After eating, Scott and Natalie were in the mood for dancing. The music was playing lively but no one was dancing so they decided to remain seated, enjoying each other's company. Inell and Thomas were having a great time; they said hello to Natalie and thanked her again for her poem. Inell had Natalie's card in her hands and told her:

"Thomas and I will never forget you Natalie, you are very thoughtful and intelligent. Your words are sincere. It was true what you said, your are never happy when you say goodbye."

Rodriguez was there too and said a cordial hello to Scott. He also told Natalie,

"You are very pretty, I almost didn't recognize you."

"Thank you, you look very different to, Rodriguez."

"Oh yes, I don't look like a mechanic now." He said with an ironic smile.

Scott and Natalie were talking and laughing during the party and she felt very happy, no matter what Rodriguez thought about her. She knew that on Monday he would be gossiping about her with his friends in the factory.

The party she tried so hard to attend was a success; she had a great time with Scott who made her feel like a queen. The party lasted until about eleven o'clock. When Natalie got in Scott's car to return home, she sat a little closer to him. He took her hand and drove in silence. He drove slowly as though he didn't want to arrive. Natalie suddenly broke the silence:

"Scott, do you want to hear the poem that I was writing the other day, the one you asked me about?"

"Yes, and you didn't want to show me what you had written."

"It was impossible that day." She said with a soft voice.

"And now you can tell me?"

"Yes, and I hope you like it."

"Oh, Natalie, I would like to hear your poem. Is it something special?"

"Yes, very special for me. It is a poem in English; I don't know a lot of English, but I wrote it anyway."

The fruit punch Natalie had been drinking helped her lose her inhibitions. She started to recite with her sweet voice the poem she wrote for him a month before.

"When you arrive, all is well,

Every thing is clear,

The world is clean!

Your eyes look at me,

Like a lake, calm, blue and deep!
When your word soft and precise
Is with me, I don't need
Anything more!
When you arrive, all is well."

When she finished Scott said: "It was beautiful." Then he put his arm around her and drew her close to his body as the car floated above the city night, as Natalie felt when they drove on the expressway above downtown Miami. It was an unforgettable moment for Natalie. The big city's brilliants lights were on both sides of the expressway as far as the eye could see. It looked like a great dream. Other cars flew by them and Natalie wished the expressway would be interminable so that her dream would last forever and she could stay close to him. But all roads have to end, and Scott and Natalie arrived home at five minutes to twelve, and she felt like a modern Cinderella:

"Now she would leave one silver shoe, and would run into her house before the clock struck twelve." She felt like saying, but that would sound silly in such a premature relation.

Scott escorted her to the door and she opened the door with her key. They both entered into the little porch. The children were sleeping and the house was silent. They stopped in the middle of the porch and Scott took her by her waist, pulling her closer to his body. She felt his masculine body and his soft cologne, and she hugged him too.

"Natalie, Natalie," he said with a passionate voice, "we have been waiting for this moment a long time. Sometimes I am indifferent to you in the factory, but I am afraid people would say bad things about us. I don't want them to know about our relationship because it would be bad for both of us."

"I know Scott, but I have suffered a lot because I wasn't sure. I thought you liked Sonia."

"No, no, only you, Natalie."

"Are you sure?" She asked with her face very close to him.

"Yes, I am sure."

He hugged her tighter, looked for her mouth and kissed her. She kissed him back, and suddenly she felt in a dream, afraid of waking up suddenly and finding herself alone in her house. His arms were strong and pressed her against his body. They kissed long and passionate and Natalie lost her sense of reality. At that moment she wished to hear from his lips

"I love you." She wished that with desperation, but maybe it was too soon for him.

Then, they separated and she accompanied him to the door. The night was clear with a full moon illuminating everything outside. They could smell the scent of flowers from the garden and the grass. He came back and hugged Natalie, now under a clear night full of stars. He didn't want to go and she felt love in his arms while he was hugging her.

"My dear," he said, "you are very pretty. I always liked you; since the first moment I saw you with your red dress."

"Do you remember that day?"

"Yes, I will never forget that. I recognized you the day you went to my office for an interview."

They kissed again with love. Nobody could see them from the street and only a car passed and shone a flash of light their way, illuminating their bodies together that blended into the front yard like one more tree. Finally, they said goodbye and he drove off.

She then entered the house and closed the door. Happiness followed her into the house, and for first time Natalie thought her happiness wouldn't escape like other times. Scott told her that he would call her, but he didn't say when, or if he loved her. Perhaps he wanted to get to know her a little better. He had told her that he had two divorces and this could be something of a hindrance, especially when there are children. There were also the cultural differences that could stand in the way of love. But she knew that they could be very happy together, her woman's instinct told her. She loved him so much that she forgot her past. As she went to sleep that magic night, she realized her sweet love had arrived.

CHAPTER 21

THE DAY AFTER

THE SUN WAS UP SUNDAY when Natalie woke up. She opened the window and a cool breeze of fresh air caressed her face. It was crisp cloudless day with an incredible blue sky. She got in the shower and started singing like never before. Eugenia, Rosa and Maria were in the living room watching cartoons, and they smiled when they heard their mother singing in the bathroom.

"I think she is very happy, it has been a long time since I heard her singing like that." Rosa said.

"Yes, she is singing like a bird," Eugenia added.

When Natalie came in the living room, Maria asked her:

"Mami how was the party?"

"Very nice."

She had her head covered with a towel, and she wore a short robe.

"I can see that everything went very well with Scott because you are very happy," Rosa said.

Natalie smiled looked at her daughter and noticed her curiosity.

"Yes he was very nice to me. It was a casual party and I had a good time. Scott is marvelous."

She confessed to her daughters.

"Then, the translation that I did was good for something."

Rosa said.

"You can't imagine how much that helped me, my dear."

"But is there something between you and him?"

Maria and Rosa asked with interest.

"Not yet, I hope that with time there will be. He is a man that has been divorced two times, and he has children. I think he has a lot of thinking to do."

"I think," Rosa, added, "he shouldn't think much. You are very pretty and very nice."

"Thank you Rosa, but we never know what men are thinking, I have to wait."

Rosa was silent. She thought that her mother could be happy with Scott; he would be a good man for her. She didn't say anything more and Natalie went to her bedroom to get dressed. She had woken up late and she wanted to be ready in case Scott would want to pay her a visit.

Adrian was still sleeping in his bedroom. Natalie walked in and woke him; she kissed him, saying that it was the time to eat his breakfast. The boy looked at her with sleepy eyes.

"It is time to wake up Adrian. It is ten o'clock and I have to fix the room."

"Why, is Scott coming over?"

Adrian asked.

"I hope so, but I am not sure."

"You know mami, I like Scott because he knows how to play football, and he told me that he would teach me. I want to be the best in my team at school."

She smiled.

"I hope that he can do that, but he is very busy sometimes."

"He promised he would come to play with me, mami. He told me the other day."

"I don't know, probably he will come here today or next week."

Sunday was a long day for Natalie, waiting for Scott's call. The previous night was very passionate for both and Natalie thought that should merit a call. The girls went to a nearby park to play volleyball, and Adrian was allowed to go next door to play with his friend. Natalie was alone waiting for Scott to call. She couldn't believe that Scott had not called. Finally, she decided to take the initiative and at two o'clock she grabbed the phone nervously and began to dial the numbers carefully. A woman answered and she instinctively hung up, thinking she dialed the wrong number. She tried again and the same voice answered in English. Her hands turned cold, but she was able to regain her poise and asked for Scott calmly.

"One moment, please," she said, sounding like an operator.

Natalie thought about what Sonia had said. "A woman answers Scott's phone." She didn't know what to think, she was disconcerted. Scott answered the phone after a few minutes, which felt like an eternity to Natalie. His voice sounded normal and reassuring.

"How are you Natalie?"

"Very well, thank you," she said with a tone of voice a little cold. She didn't know what was going on, but Scott told her something reasonable that made her feel better.

"I was just going to call you now, but I was busy cutting the grass in the garden that was getting too high. And you, what have you been doing?"

"Well, not much, cleaning the house. The girls went to the park, and Adrian is playing with a friend next door."

Natalie couldn't resist the temptation to ask him about the woman who answered the phone.

"Do you have a visitor Scott?"

He sounded surprised by her question.

"No, I don't have a visitor, the children are with me today."

Natalie hesitated for a moment, she felt bad and wished that she had not called, but she did and now she had to know. She could not go ahead with the doubt in her mind making her suffer. It was better to discover the truth, but she had to use discretion because in reality the night before could have been simply a date for him. She talked very soft as though not to bother him.

"I thought you had a visitor because somebody else answered the phone."

She said trying to demonstrate indifference. She was very nervous, but his answer was reassuring and natural:

"Oh, that was Betty."

At that moment, Natalie wanted to hang up the phone because she couldn't find the courage to ask him "who is Betty?" He didn't say anything about her. She was silent on the other end of the line, waiting for him to make it clear who Betty was so she would tell him goodbye. Natalie's English vocabulary was not extensive and her nerves were altered with doubt.

"Hello Natalie, are you there?"

"Yes," she said with a soft voice that Scott almost couldn't hear.

"Why don't you talk to me?"

"I was waiting for you to tell me who Betty was?" She couldn't avoid this question.

Suddenly, she heard him laugh, happy, juvenile and sincere.

"Betty is my baby-sitter. She comes here to take care of the children sometimes."

Natalie stayed silent for a moment, thinking how stupid she had been.

"Oh God, how much I have suffered for a couple of minutes! It is Sonia's fault because she put that doubt in my mind," she thought.

"Oh, I thought she was a friend." She finally said.

"Natalie, I told you that I don't have any guests."

"Excuse me, but I didn't know about your babysitter. When will you bring the children to my house?"

She said trying to change the subject. She felt bad that he might think she was jealous.

"Next Sunday," he said, "today it is a little complicated. Yesterday I couldn't do anything. I had to wash my car and change the oil."

"I see, I just wanted to know how you were doing"

She said with a soft voice. She didn't say anything about the night before, but he did.

"We had a very lovely time last night, didn't we?"

"Yes Scott, very nice."

She wanted to say that she wished to see him, to be in his arms again, but she wouldn't. Their relationship was just starting and she didn't feel confident enough. He may wait a little longer to get to know her better because in reality he didn't know anything about her. He only knew her as an employee, besides she didn't even speak his language very well. But for now she felt better knowing he was not married like Sonia maliciously told her. Scott was a sincere man; she saw that in his clear eyes. If he would tell her about his love, it would be from the bottom of his heart. She was sure about that.

She sighed again and then said: "Goodbye Scott" you are very busy now."

"No, not too busy." He said.

"Yes, I know, we are going to see each other tomorrow."

Their goodbye was normal. Nothing related to the passionate kisses and hugs of the night before was mentioned. Natalie thought for a moment that Americans were probably different, and that they must suffer from partial amnesia to forget things like that. Natalie was very sentimental, one moment she was happy, the next she was sad. Now she couldn't help feeling disappointed because Scott didn't mention their passionate night.

The following day Natalie arrived at the factory very excited. She wore new jeans and makeup, which she almost never did when she went to work. She thought, "I am going to see him, and I am supposed to look pretty." She was walking fast, and said hello to her friends with unusual cheerfulness. Teresa was at her machine and smiled at Natalie, but they couldn't talk because she had to get everything ready at her machine in ten minutes before the bell rang. Natalie looked around to check if Scott was there, but couldn't see him anywhere in the factory. He was probably in his office, Natalie thought.

She started to cut open some boxes with a knife when Scott passed by. She moved a little to see him, and for a second she lost concentration and accidentally cut herself on her finger. Blood came out and she screamed in pain. Scott realized what happened, but instead of coming to help her, he ordered Tidra to bring the First aid kit and take care of Natalie's wound. The forelady quickly brought antiseptic, cotton and adhesive bandages. The injury was superficial and Tidra took care of it quickly.

"What happened to you Natalie?" she asked

"I was opening this box and I cut my finger, I don't know how."

"You have to pay more attention, especially when you are working with a sharp
knife."

"Yes, thank you, I don't think it is too bad."

"Are you able to work?"

"Sure, that's not a problem."

But Natalie had a problem, she was sad because Scott was ignoring her even when she needed some help. Any boss would have come to her employee's aid, but not him.

"Well, another dream gone with the wind." She thought to her self. Natalie was disenchanted the rest of the day, and she didn't feel like talking to her friends about Inel's party anymore. To top it off, Rodriguez appeared with his ironic smile.

"Oh Natalie, it looked like you had a great time Saturday night."

"You too Rodriguez, with your wife, I hope."

She answered without smiling.

"I have to be with my wife, what do you think?"

"I don't think anything, but I don't know your wife. You never introduced her to me."

"But you were very busy with your American and didn't pay any attention to other people."

She felt like insulting him, but she did what he hated the most: she ignored him and walked away.

CHAPTER 22

WARREN

THE WEEK AFTER THE INJURY incident, Natalie waited in vane for Scott to talk to her or call her on the phone. One afternoon he walked by her machine and stopped to say hello to Sonia and her, and then he went to another machine. Natalie understood he couldn't jeopardize his job by showing favoritism, but he could at least call her at night. She couldn't comprehend why he had stopped in the middle of the way; why all of the sudden he was not interested in her anymore. She couldn't find an answer.

In another department of the factory there was a man named Warren. He was a very attractive, young American guy. He always looked at Natalie when he passed near her machine. Teresa noticed it and told her:

"That man likes you."

"No, he doesn't, he only says hello to me sometimes. He is good looking isn't he?" Natalie said smiling.

"Yes he is, but I don't like American men,"

Teresa said smiling. She was married to a Latin man and had two children.

"I do like American men." Natalie said.

"You'd better don't like Warren because Tidra told me he is married."

"Sometimes she makes mistakes, she said that Scott was a bad boss and he is the best we ever had."

"You are right about that, probably Scott is the man you need. I think Warren likes every woman."

Natalie looked at her friend surprised.

"What did you say about Scott?"

For a moment she thought that Teresa knew about their short-lived relationship.

"Nothing, he is divorced and so are you. Besides he likes you. Tidra told me that both of you had a good time at that party."

"Yes, but that doesn't mean anything, we are just friends."

At that moment Rodriguez passed by, and the two friends fell silent. She wanted to avoid hearing another of his bad and malicious jokes. She was trying hard not to be rude to him. After Teresa went to her machine and Natalie was alone, Rodriguez asked her:

"Have you seen your dear boss again? I didn't know you liked Americans."

Natalie looked at him very seriously and answered.

"Please Rodriguez, it is not your business. Scott is my friend, that's all."

"Yes, between friend and boyfriend there is a short distance."

She couldn't answer him because he walked away with a malicious smile on his face.

Friday afternoon Warren came by and stopped at Natalie's machine. He stood close to her and pretended he was looking at the bags coming out of the machine. He casually asked Natalie for her name. She had never seen him up close; he had green eyes and light brown hair. He was handsome. She looked at him, smiling.

"My name is Natalie."

"Natalie is a pretty name. Do you know that for a long time I have wanted to talk to you, but you are always very serious. I didn't know if you would talk to me"

She smiled again,

"Do you think I am very serious?"

"Yes, I pass by every morning and I try to say hello, but you don't seem to want to look at me."

"I never notice when you go by. I was always very busy with the machine. If I don't pay attention the bags would end up on the floor."

They both smiled and without wasting any time he asked her out.

"Do you want to go out with me tonight?"

"I don't know; I have to think about it."

She said, trying to size up the situation. He insisted.

"We can go to dinner and dancing later. Do you like to dance?"

"Yes, I like to dance, but it is better that you call me on the phone first, I cannot decide now."

He looked at her closely, smiling as if he has made a conquest. By now his unexpected visit to Natalie was getting noticed by other operators and a superior who was passing by. That person happened to be Scott. Warren was writing Natalie's telephone number and address on a piece of paper. Scott hesitated for a moment and observed the man who was close to Natalie on the opposite side of Sonia. He didn't say anything, but he frowned in disapproval. He wasn't supposed to be talking to operators when they were working; they both knew that. He walked fast toward his office. Natalie saw him passing by, but she pretended she was distracted and smiled coquettishly at Warren. The game she started was very old, but it was worth trying. She thought.

Scott sat at his desk and started to revise the papers that he had to fill out with the day's production. He wrote the numbers fast, showing how the operators did that day. The production was not bad. He wanted to leave early that day. Everyday he has been working late, until seven or eight at night. He felt angry and lit a cigarette. He didn't smoke in the plant because it was prohibited for the employees, but he could smoke in his office. He inhaled the smoke trying to erase from his mind something that bothered him and interrupted his concentration. Then, he stood up and looked through the window where he could see the plant. He stood on one side of the window and watched. Warren was still at Natalie's machine, talking to her. She was smiling while picking up the bags adeptly. He contemplated her pretty face with attractive features, and her soft skin.

Then, in a very unusual move Scott left the papers unfinished and went down to the plant. He walked around, observing how the machines were running. He said hello to the operators who were working on the left side, and went directly to Natalie who was working closing some boxes while Pedro changed the roll on the machine. He stopped close to her and he looked at her smiling. She was a little surprised to see him.

"How are you, Natalie?" he said.

"Very well thank you, and you Scott?"

"Pretty good. We haven't talked for many days. I have been very busy working late almost every night. How are your children?"

"Very good," she answered.

Natalie didn't say anything more. She went ahead closing the boxes with tape. He stood there, breaking the company's rules. He looked at her with passionate expression in his eyes. She felt a little nervous because of the look in his eyes.

"Listen Natalie," he said with his soft voice that she loved. "I would like to visit you this afternoon. I will try to leave early today. Do you think six o'clock would be Okay?"

"Yes, sure."

She answered, forgetting completely that she had been talking to Warren about an invitation. Even worse—he could pay her a visit that night.

CHAPTER 23

THE RESTAURANT

THAT AFTERNOON NATALIE ASKED PEDRO if he could take her home. She wanted to arrive early so she would have enough time to take a shower and dress nicely for Scott. He was coming at six o'clock.

"I don't pass by your house, but I will take you if you want me to."

"Thank you, Pedro, I only need a ride today."

"We don't go dancing today?"

"No, it is impossible, I have a guest coming this afternoon, that's why I want to arrive home early."

Pedro made a gesture and said,

"Natalie, you are killing me with your things. Now you want me to take you home because you have a date with another man. What about me?"

"You have a very pretty wife, remember?"

He smiled and nodded.

"Who is the lucky guy?"

She didn't answer. They were good friends and he knew that she loved Scott.

Slowed by the rush-hour traffic, they arrived at her house at five thirty. She had half an hour to take a shower and be presentable. Suddenly she remembered Warren and she panicked. He said something about coming to visit her that night.

"Oh God! What did I do?"

Flirting with Warren may have pushed Scott to act, but now she was in trouble. If the two men arrived at the same time to her house, she could loose both of them. She had to do something quick. She called Rosa to help her. The girl looked at her surprised because her mother was very nervous.

"Dear, you have to help me, Eugenia and Maria you too." She said.

"What happened mother?" Rosa said, "Do you need another translation?"

"No, it is something else very delicate."

She went ahead and explained how she flirted with Warren to get Scott's attention.

` "Tonight it's possible that both of them would show up here."

"Why did you do that?" Rosa asked very seriously.

"I thought Scott would never talk to me again, and I smiled at Warren when he was passing by."

"Oh, I understand, you wanted to make Scott jealous with the other man."

Rosa said

"Did you do that mami?" Eugenia inquired.

"Yes, and later Scott came to my machine and asked me if he could come to visit me this afternoon."

"I have to change my clothes and be ready in a half hour."

"What do you plan to do about that other man, Warren?"

"I don't know, it is possible that he will call me on the phone first. If he does that, you tell him that I left to see a sick friend and will come back late. I will go out with Scott to the park and will come back late. I cannot be here because I am afraid Warren might show up."

"What a problem you have, it is your fault mami,"

Rosa insisted.

"If Warren comes here, what are we supposed to do?"

"Don't let him in. Tell him that I went out and will come back late, that's all you have to say."

Rosa was a little disappointed and told her mother, don't try to play with two men again because you could loose Scott.

"Yes dear, I know, but I had to do something so that Scott would make a decision, and I couldn't think of any other way of doing it. You are very young and you don't understand that sometimes we have to bet everything on one card."

"Mami, don't talk to me figuratively; I understand more than you think. Anyway I don't like what you did."

Natalie looked at her and smiled with sweetness; her daughter was an intelligent and serious girl. She was right, she wasn't supposed to act like that.

"Would you please help me?"

She asked her daughters.

"Sure mami, we are going to be ready to answer the phone. And in case the man comes, what does he look like mom?"

Maria wanted to know.

"He is tall, has green eyes and he is young."

Natalie kissed the girls and went to the bathroom to take a shower.

Scott arrived at six o'clock, as expected. He came with his work clothes on and looked a little tired. She looked pretty and rejuvenated after her shower with her hair clean, bright and sweet scented. She welcomed him with a smile without mentioning the sad days she had been going through without talking to him. The girls said hello to Scott very friendly. Adrian came running from the yard to see him and ask him when he would teach him to play good football.

"On Sunday, I will bring my children so that you can see them."

Scott answered.

"All right! Adrian celebrated.

Natalie was nervous about what happened with Warren and the possibility that he could come to her house. After a few tense moments in the house, she told him:

"Scott would you like to go to the park again? It is a little hot here."

"Where ever you want to go. I am sorry that I couldn't change my cloths, but I live far and it is difficult to come back here."

He excused himself.

"Oh don't worry Scott you look great."

"Yes, very sweaty; today I was working with the old machines. They don't want to change anything, and then they want good production. They have only one mechanic who doesn't care about fixing them properly. He gives me the impression that he wants me out of the factory."

For the first time Scott talked to Natalie about his problems in the factory. Maybe this was the reason why he couldn't visit her more frequently. She felt a bit guilty for being inpatient and failing to understand his problems at work.

"Yes," she said, "Rodriguez has not forgiven the owners for replacing him. You should talk with them about him."

He didn't answer, but he looked like he was considering Natalie's suggestion.

After that conversation they left the house, and they went to the park. They sat in the same place they did the first time. There were some couples around and children playing. The big trees covered the sun, and the afternoon breeze messed up Natalie's hair. Scott smelled her perfume, making him move closer to her.

"My sweetheart I missed you a lot, you don't know how much." He said.

"I missed you too, Scott. I thought you weren't going to talk to me anymore."

"Why do you say that?"

"I saw you from a distance, but you didn't see me. You looked as though you regretted everything."

"Regret what, Natalie?"

"Well, I don't know, I cannot explain. You may be able to figure it out yourself."

He hugged her then. He smelled of cologne and oil from the machines, but Natalie felt so happy that she didn't care.

"Natalie, if you only knew how many times I thought of you. It is difficult to explain, I am very busy checking everything in the factory and sometimes I cannot go to talk to you. I wished I could my love."

They hugged under the big trees and kissed passionately. The passion was mutual and their bodies were together for a long time. Natalie's complaints about Scott and all her problems suddenly vanished. When somebody walked by them Natalie tried to separate her body from him, but Scott wouldn't let her. It seemed like he wanted to make up for the lost time. This unforgettable afternoon flew by and suddenly night covered everything. Mosquitoes made their unwanted appearance, bringing them back to reality.

She looked at her watch; it was seven thirty at night. She remembered Warren, and she felt scared. It was unlikely that Warren would be waiting for her at her house.

"Sweetheart," Scott said. "I think we must go back to your house. It is dark and the mosquitoes are vicious. I am going to call the city and ask them to send people here to fumigate this park."

"Yes Scott, it is better that we go back now."

"Tonight I have to go home early because with these clothes I can't invite you anywhere, but tomorrow we will go some place. I will call you on the phone."

When they arrived home Natalie looked nervously, looking for Warren's car, but to her relieve there was no car.

They said goodbye in the garden with a casual kiss because Natalie's daughters might be looking out the window, waiting for her. He kissed her soft lips and promised again to call tomorrow morning. Natalie entered the house and found her children watching the TV.

"What happened with Warren?" She asked immediately.

"He called," Rosa said, "we told him you were not here; that's all."

"That's it?"

"Yes," Maria said, "the only problem is that we don't have dinner. Rosa and Eugenia didn't prepare anything and I am very hungry."

Natalie laughed.

"Don't worry, I will cook something in a moment."

The following morning the phone rang at nine o'clock. Natalie answered quickly because she was waiting for Scott's call.

"Hello," she said.

A masculine voice answered:

"How are you Natalie?"

"I am okay, thank you, and you?"

"Very well. I called you very early because I want to go to the beach, if we go later the beach will be too crowded. Do you want to go with me?"

"Oh yes," she said happy to hear Scott's voice. "Will you bring your children today?"

He was silent for a moment.

"Natalie, I don't have any children. I think you confused my voice with another man, and I know who he is."

At that point she realized she had been talking to Warren.

Obviously, this was the end of Natalie's friendship with Warren, but she was happy because that day Scott came to visit her with his two sons. They were very handsome, blond hair and blue eyes like their father. Little Scott was seven years old; Sean was five. She kissed them and Sean returned her kiss, but Scott did not, he just looked at her with intelligent eyes and smiled. Later they all went to the beach, and Maria and Adrian were very happy playing with Scott's boys. The weather was perfect with a bright sun accentuating the turquoise waters of Miami Beach. Natalie's heart palpitated fast when Scott saw her in her bathing suit. She noticed he was impressed by her body. He took her by her waist and very sweet told Natalie:

"You are very beautiful Natalie."

"You are very handsome too."

She answered a little shy, looking at his strong muscles. He smiled and noticed that she liked him too. The children were very happy at the beach, playing with the waves and the ball that Scott brought for them. Adrian was swimming and body surfing, and Scott told him not to go out too far. Maria looked very beautiful in her bikini, and she lay down on the beach to get a tan.

Life was good that day. At five o'clock Scott called the children to go back. He told Natalie he would like to invite her out to eat. Natalie was very happy and nervous at the same time. She didn't have a new dress to wear that night, which would be the appropriate thing to do considering the occasion. However, she said yes. It may still be possible for her to buy a new dress. She could ask Irma to take her to the mall. It was a favor worth asking for. As far as she could tell this was going to be their night.

The Candilejas Restaurant was expectedly full on that Saturday night. It was an elegant place with a terrace overlooking Biscayne Bay. Lights of many colors illuminated the beautiful front garden with the right amount of brightness. Scott had made reservations, so they were immediately led to their table on the second floor. The table Scott had reserved was on the terrace with full view to the bay. He knew that Natalie loved the ocean. Scott was wearing an elegant gray suit, and Natalie's new dress was gorgeous. She was very pretty that night with the smile of a very happy woman. From their table they could see the vastness of the bay. It was a breath taking scenery doted by lights from shimmering ships, set against the backdrop of Miami's skyline. Natalie was silent for a moment, mesmerized by the magic of the ambiance. Scott took her hand with love and they both felt the same happy sensation. A fresh breeze from the infinite sea accompanied Sinatra's Fly Me to the Moon, playing in the background.

Scott had ordered a bottle of champagne. They made a toast, looking into each other's eyes.

"To us," he said.

"To our love," she replied.

At that moment Natalie was the happiest woman in the world. The foam of the champagne overflowed the cups and they laughed, drinking a little and kissing.

"This is beautiful," Natalie, said, "I will never forget this night."

"I am glad you are enjoying this place. I tried to find a place by the water, I know you like the ocean."

"Thanks, I am very happy like never before in my life."

Natalie was referring more to their growing love than to the magic of the place. Later the waiter arrived with their dinner: grilled shrimp for Scott, and a fillet of fish for Natalie. Dinner was served on fine China, adorned with fresh lettuce. They eat slowly; flavoring each bite, each zip of champagne, every kiss. The night was one of those perfect moments in someone's life to be cherished forever.

CHAPTER 24

HAPPY TIMES

NEXT MORNING SCOTT CAME BACK to Natalie's house with his two boys. Scott looked younger in shorts, t-shirt and tennis shoes. He kissed her and they were all smiles. Adrian came running to see the boys and invited them to play in the yard. Later they went to the park to play baseball. Rosa stayed at home studying for the next day. Eugenia went out with a friend. They all participated in the game. Little Scott tried to hit the ball, but he missed most of the time and this made him angry and threw away the bat. Adrian tried to explain to him he would get better with practice, but he sat down under the trees and saying,

"I am not going to play anymore".

Scott looked at him and warned him,

"If you continue with this attitude we wont play anymore and I will take you back home."

The boy looked at him and noticed that his daddy was serious.

Natalie intervened,

"Don't worry; children are like that, they don't like to lose."

Scott didn't agree and told her that he had to listen. After a while, little Scott came back to play with Adrian and Maria.

They returned to her house in the afternoon. Rosa helped Natalie prepare a hearty dinner for all. She cooked chicken with rice, cornbread and salad.

"Dinner was delicious,"

Scott celebrated, after eating with a good appetite. His boys, however, did not eat much.

"They are not used to the Latin seasoning," Natalie said.

"They will learn with time," Scott answered.

Natalie liked Scott's words and smiled. Rosa and Maria smiled too, thinking that the friendship between Scott and their mother was serious. Natalie had changed her clothes and was now wearing a yellow dress, short and sexy. Scott did not spare an opportunity to admire her when she walked by to tend to the table. At eight o'clock Scott stood up and announced he had to take the children back. He called his children who were watching television with Adrian. Natalie walked them outside to say goodbye. When they were out on the front yard, Scott took Natalie's hand and asked her:

"Do you want to go with us? I have to take them back to their mother's house. I will bring you back at about ten o'clock."

She looked at him surprised. He had never invited her to go with him to see his house, much less to visit his ex-wife. This worried her a little, but she thought maybe she could in the car when they got there. She agreed and walked back into the house to tell Rosa and Maria to take care of Adrian, and that she would come back soon.

"Mami, Maria said, "Where are you going?"

"I am going with Scott to take his children back home."

"Please come home early,"

Adrian said. She kissed them and went back to Scott. She was emotional, a little scared, but happy. It was a long drive and the boys fell as sleep in the car, being tired from a long day. That gave them an opportunity to talk in private. He took her hand with his right arm and pulled her closer to him. When they stopped at a red light he kissed her. His caresses were passionate and Natalie responded with all her love.

"I would like to find many red lights along the way so we could kiss at every stop."

He said, smiling.

They both laughed and during the trip they stopped three more times at red lights and kissed passionately, oblivious to other cars.

Finally they arrived at the condo where the children were living with their mother. Scott woke the children up and opened the door to Natalie.

"I can wait here."

She said, trying to avoid meeting a woman who may not be very happy to see her.

"No, I have to talk to Christine, and I don't want you to be here alone. Come Natalie, please."

They walked to the entrance of the apartment. It was a nice building located in a good neighborhood. The children took off running and when they got there, they rang the doorbell. Soon somebody opened the door. It was a woman tall and blond, but at that moment Natalie couldn't see her face. The children entered the apartment in a hurry and she said something in English that Natalie couldn't understand. The lady didn't kiss them or welcome them with love. Natalie stopped in front of the door that was half way open. Scott introduced them:

"Natalie this is Christine. Christine this is Natalie."

Natalie smiled and said,

"I am glad to met you."

Christine mumbled something between her teeth, and she turned away from the door to let Natalie in. She had a strong body and a face with defined features, but not pretty. Her eyes were big, blue, very deep and cold. Natalie couldn't determine her age, but perceived her indifference. She noticed that she didn't like her presence in her house. Scott asked Natalie to sit down, and he walked upstairs with Christine. The children followed them. Natalie decided to look around the house. The living room was nicely decorated, with a few pieces of furniture of good quality. She observed that she had good paintings on the walls, but no plants or flowers around. There were some fine pieces of German porcelain on the center of a table. She felt like an intruder in the house, but she thought that it would only be for a short time. Christine was divorced from Scott, but she ignored the reasons behind it. After several minutes Natalie started to become a little anxious being alone in the small living room, when she heard their footsteps coming down the stairs. Scott excused himself for taking too long. Christine came down behind him, and Natalie listened when the children asked if they could come down too, she said that they should go to bed immediately. The woman passed by her side without looking at her and she started to pickup some things from the table. There were glasses, cups and papers on the table; it looked like she had been writing. She ignored Natalie completely, which made Natalie feel so bad that she wished she had not entered the apartment. She felt better when Scott said that they had to go. She said good night, but Christine didn't answer.

When Scott and Natalie got into to the car she wanted to say something to him, but she thought that it would be better to keep silent. She felt bad being ignored by his ex wife without an explanation. There was nothing between them anymore, except their children, so Natalie couldn't understand her unfriendliness.

"What happened sweetheart, why are you so silent?"

"I was thinking Scott, only thinking."

"What were you thinking about?"

He asked in a soft voice.

"About us."

She said, looking at the faraway lights of the city that always inspired owe in her with their magic reflections. City lights in the United States seemed surprisingly brighter and more abundant; they were never so intense back in her hometown. Scott was silent for a moment. Maybe he was thinking of them too. He took her delicate hands that were cold and caressed them with his big warm hands. She felt protected when she was close to him. She felt a sense of security every time she was with him because she now loved him and trusted him. They drove off and Natalie got lost in her thoughts. Suddenly, she noticed that they had left the expressway and were driving through a neighborhood unfamiliar to her. She figured it was close to the sea because she could smell it in the air. The houses appeared modern and very big with impeccably manicured gardens all around. She was curious about where they were going and asked Scott:

"What is this place, Scott?"

"This is part of Miami Shores. You have never been here before?"

"No, I really don't know Miami very well. I am always busy and besides I don't have a car."

"Yes, I know."

Scott didn't say anything else and went ahead driving slowly through the solitary streets. It was ten o'clock at night. She didn't ask him where they were going because she thought he wanted to show her around before taking her back home. Unexpectedly, he stopped his car in front of a house. It was a sumptuous house for Natalie, surrounded by big trees that were projecting shadows over the driveway. She was surprised and thought that he wanted to visit some friends. Then she asked:

"Whose house is this, Scott?"

Still with his hands on the steering wheel, he smiled softly and answered,

"This is my house Natalie, do you want go with me to see it?"

"Your house Scott?" she asked astonished, "but it is very big and pretty. You told me that you were looking for an apartment, remember?"

"Yes, that was before I got to know you. I was thinking of selling, because it is too big for a man alone."

Natalie fell silent for a moment.

Don't you want to go in my love?" He asked.

"Yes Scott, I would like to see your house."

"But you are very quiet. I am sorry that I didn't bring you here before, but there was always something.

Scott and Natalie walked through the front yard holding hands. The garden looked meticulously kept. Under the dim light of the moon, Scott's house seemed surreal to Natalie. The trees around the house moved like ghosts in the wind, casting distorted shadows on the garden. The sweet smell of an unfamiliar flower blended with the gentle ocean breeze to confuse her senses. They walked into the front porch and she was marveled by the tropical feeling of the place. Plants and vines covered part of the walls; bamboo furniture reminded her of her Caribbean past; toys were strewn on the floor.

Scott turned on the outside lights and the entire majestic splendor of the house came into being. It was an old Spanish-style house rich in architectural details. He turned to her saying:

"You are very silent, dear?"

"I am so surprised Scott, I didn't think that you had a house so pretty, you never told me about it."

"This is actually a very modest home; any middle-class family could buy it."

He hugged her and told her:

"It is your house too Natalie. Take the key, you can open it; everything mine is yours too."

"I don't know Scott," she said in a soft voice, "I don't know what to say, it is marvelous."

"Not really; it is a little old house with a lot of work to be done. I have to do some repairs."

"It is beautiful, I love it."

"But if you don't go in, you won't know what it is like inside. Take the key my love."

His voice was very passionate like never before. She took the key and opened the door. Everything was dark inside and Scott turned the light on, illuminating the living room. It was very spacious with big utilitarian furniture. There were many white cushions on the sofa and chairs. The wood floors were partially covered with Persian rugs. The walls were decorated with paintings, which appeared to be original. Sheer curtains covered the windows and some natural plants grew in pots. Natalie was surprised to find out that Scott lived in such a beautiful house.

"Dear, what happened? You are so quiet. Don't you like it? As I said earlier, forgive me for not bringing you here before, but I didn't find the moment, and there was always something that got in the way."

"You are very rich Scott I didn't know that," she said with sadness. "I am poor and I have a big family."

"What are you talking about Natalie?" I am not rich. Anybody with a good job can buy this house. Besides I still have many years to pay for this house."

She finally smiled as they sat on the sofa. They hugged with passion and Natalie forgot about everything, except that she was happy in his arms. Later, Scott brought a bottle of wine and two glasses.

"To you, Natalie, for being in my life." He said.

"To you my love, forever." She answered.

They drank the wine and then continued to hug forgetting everything else. Natalie forgot that she told her children that she would come back home by ten o'clock. The splendid moment with sweet love had arrived, and she was floating in a world of happiness she never knew before.

"My love do you want to go to the second floor?"

"Yes, I want to go with you."

They went up the stairway that was covered with green carpeting leading to the bedrooms. Scott took her by her waist and kissed her hair.

"Natalie, we have been waiting a long time for this, I think it's time to be together, nothing can separate us."

"Yes, Scott, nothing or nobody can separate us."

The second floor, like the rest of the house, was simple but nicely decorated. There were three bedrooms with closed doors, apparently because nobody was using them.

"This is my bedroom."

He said, as he opened the door to one of the rooms. The bedroom was big and the window was open. Natalie walked close to the window and felt the sea freeze.

"Can you see the ocean form here?"

"No but you can feel it in the air."

The bedroom was neatly organized with a king-size bed covered by a colorful comforter. The few pieces of furniture appeared to be antique.

"Scott," she said, "I love you. But I have been suffering thinking that you didn't love me."

"Natalie, I love you, I always will. I loved you since the first moment I saw you walking with your red dress that looked so nice on you, which, by the way, I haven't seen since that first occasion."

"I will wear it everyday if you like." She answered laughingly.

They hugged again with a passion they couldn't control anymore. He kissed her mouth, her face, and he said suddenly:

"Natalie, I love you, I love you!"

Finally he said what Natalie had been waiting for a long time. Scott softly opened the zipper on Natalie's dress, and her dress fell to the floor. The pale light that entered through the window illuminated her entire body. Then he said softly:

"How beautiful you are my dear."

Natalie didn't answer but she saw his handsome body with strong muscles. Then, he asked her:

"Are you sure you want to stay with me, Natalie"

"Yes, I am, tonight and always."

When Natalie woke up, the antique clock on Scott's bedside table stroke 5:15 am. She panicked; her children had been alone all night. She told them she was going to come back by 10 P.M. She looked at Scott and he was sleeping placidly next to her. She reassured herself,

"I am very happy and this couldn't wait any longer."

She kissed his face very softly and he moved a little.

"My love," she said trying to wake him up. "I have to go back home. My children don't need to know that I have been out all night."

He hugged and kissed her again, murmuring,

"don't worry my love, they have to understand."

"Yes, but I have to talk with them. I cannot do this because it could set a bad example."

"Stop worrying and go back to sleep, we will be married soon."

She heard that but disregarded it because he was half asleep. She was sure he would not remember later. She got dressed and combed her hair in the bathroom hurriedly. She thought it was better not to wake him up. She could take a taxi. She took her purse and ran downstairs. The lights were still on in the living room. As she was leaving through the front porch, she heard Scott screaming through the bedroom window.

"Wait Natalie, wait for me, I will take you home."

She went back into the house and waited for him on the sofa. After a few minutes he came down still buttoning up his shirt.

"How impatient you are my love."

They looked at each other under the living room lights and laughed, hugged and kissed. It was still dark when they left. There wasn't a lot of traffic and they arrived at Natalie's house thirty minutes later. The lights were not on and Natalie felt relieved that the children were still sleeping. She said goodbye to him at the entrance of the garden. Scott hugged her tightly and said:

"I love you."

She said the same and kissed him.

"Tonight I will come back to see you."

Natalie went inside, still enveloped in an aura of happiness and turmoil. She checked Adrian's room, then the girls' and everybody was sound asleep. She felt like she had been gone for a long time. It was the first time she arrived in the morning to her house.

CHAPTER 25

UNEXPECTED PROPOSAL

THAT NIGHT SCOTT CAME BACK with a bouquet of red flowers for Natalie. He kissed her on her cheek because the children were looking at them. He was very elegant, and Natalie was wearing the blue dress that she wore at Inel's party. She thanked Scott and went to the kitchen to look for a vase to put the roses in. Meanwhile, Scott stayed in the living room talking to Eugenia, Rosa, Maria and Adrian who were all looking at him silently.

"Do you think the flowers are pretty?" he asked them.

"Beautiful,"

Rosa and Maria said at the same time.

"Do you think your mother likes them?"

Maria laughed while looking at Rosa.

"Yes my mother is very happy."

And you are happy too, do you like me?" Scott asked.

The three girls smiled timidly because they understood the depth of the question. There was definitely something serious between their mother and him. Rosa answered with her characteristic mature attitude, like an older person:

"Yes Scott, we like you."

He smiled and sat on the sofa. Then he turned to Adrian, who was looking at him with his big eyes very attentive.

"How about you Adrian, what do you say, do you like me?"

"Oh yes, you play football very good."

They all laughed. Natalie came back with the beautiful roses and put the vase on the center of the table.

Later that evening, Scott invited Natalie to go out for dinner. This time he invited her to Les Violines, an elegant and trendy restaurant. Scott ordered champagne. They toasted again to their happiness, present and future. He was particularly happy and excited that night, especially after a few glasses of champagne.

"Today I didn't go to work, I couldn't. I was sleeping and dreaming of you."

He finished with a smile. She took his hand and kissed it with love.

"Why did you do that?" She asked.

"Because you have made me very happy."

"No more than you have made me, I want to stay with you forever. You know Scott, sometimes I think I am dreaming and I am afraid to wake up in the factory under the perverse look of Rodriguez, screaming that he will fire me for writing poems."

"Don't say that sweetheart. Try to forget about that. Now everything is going to be different."

Then, he took her delicate hand and kissed it.

"My dear Natalie, would you marry me?"

He asked unexpectedly with a soft voice. She listened but in a dream-like state, unable to answer. She had been waiting to hear those words for a long time, but now she was afraid of waking up in her lonely bed, and then having to run to the corner on a cold morning to take the bus. She would then go to a dreadful factory where monstrous machines ran nonstop all the time into eternity, producing bags that she must organize and pack. Nobody can save her from the machine, not even Scott.

"Dear did you hear me? Don't you want to marry me?"

"Oh Scott, my love, yes! I want to marry you, I thought that I was still dreaming."

"No sweetheart, look I brought this for you."

He pulled a little box from his pocket and opened it. The diamond engagement ring was bright even in the dim light of the restaurant.

"Give me your hand please, I want to put it on your finger. I hope it is the right size."

She extended her hand, and he put the ring on, smiling with pride.

"It is perfect for me. It is very beautiful, it must have cost you a lot."

"Nothing is to expensive for you, my love."

"Thank you Scott, this is most happy day of my life."

She said in her not-so-perfect English, looking at the ring.

"You will be happier when we are married. I want to marry you in three months. Earlier I was talking to your daughters and your son. And they told me that they liked me. I don't think they will be a problem between us."

"No there won't be any problems, you are a very good man."

"I am not perfect, Natalie. Maybe with your placid temperament you can teach me to be happy. In the beginning I had doubts because I don't want to divorce ever again. I have been married two times, and I feel like I can't take another divorce."

"No, this will not happen again, you know I love you with all my heart, and we won't have any reason to separate ever. Sometimes I think that I have to understand more English because the language difference is a barrier that I cannot pass. I love you, and would feel very bad that you could say something I interpret in another way or vise versa."

He listened to her intently while she was trying to explain her thoughts.

She was convinced that she needed to improve her English to get out of that vicious circle she was in. She was intelligent, sensitive and wanted to get ahead in her new life, especially for her children. It has been three long and hard years since she arrived in Miami and now her life was about to change for the better. She has managed to survive as an illegal immigrant with her four children, earning minimum wages and living under the constant threat of deportation. Any mistake or report from disgruntled coworker could send the dreadful Inmigración (Immigration and Naturalization Services) after her and her children. In fact, she had worked out a secret code with her children to warn her. If Immigration officials were waiting for her in her house, the children were instructed to take a plant pot out and place it next to the front door.

"Listen Natalie, when we are married, you wont' have to work anymore. You will leave the factory and go to school if you like. You are perfect for me, you don't need anything to make me happy, but I know you wish to study and get ahead in this country so you can study and improve your English."

"Scott," she said surprised, "did you say I will leave the factory to study?" It is not possible; I have to work for my children. You cannot do it alone with all the expenses."

He smiled and answered:

"Yes dear, I have a small house, but we can all fit. Believe me, it is not a burden to help your lovely family."

"Are you sure, Scott?" She asked inquisitively. "I don't want us to have a problem because of this."

"No my love, I can do it."

He answered in a reassuring tone.

"Thank you Scott, you have made me very happy. For sure some day I will get a good job and you will be proud of me."

"I am proud of you now, you don't know how much."

She smiled and her eyes lighted up with happiness. She looked like another woman, different, attractive, distinguished, with a lively personality; very different from the sad woman she had been. Scott's words had rescued her from the hostile world she fell in. Now he trusted her. Her past life suddenly looked remote and blurry. She understood that the words of a loving man could elevate or sink a woman. The male voices of the past that echoed in her ears for so long began to dissipate: "I feel bad when I am with you" or "You take me to the worst places." Her engagement ring glittered on her finger. The man of her life looked at her with love; she didn't have anything to worry about. The sad voices of the past had to die with everything that had made her suffer.

CHAPTER 26

THE WEDDING

ONE WEEK BEFORE NATALIE AND Scott's wedding, everyone at the factory already knew about it. Natalie had invited some friends to a small party that was going to take place at Scott's house. Most people at the factory were very surprised about the news, especially Rodriguez who never expected Scott to marry an operator. It was simply unheard of in the factory.

It was the end of August, and Miamians were desperately awaiting the cooler weather of autumn. Summer had been particularly hot and rainy. The sky was partially cloudy and the wind was blowing timidly through Natalie's front yard, playing with fallen leaves. It was a hot but beautiful day and the sun penetrated through the open windows of Natalie's house. Happiness was palpable in every corner of the house. The girls were very exited, making the small pink-and-blue flowers for the guests to the wedding. They were talking about how their life would be when they move to Scott's house. Adrian was happy too, playing in the backyard. Their mother was out buying things for their wedding and a pair of roller skates for Adrian. Their life was about to change. The children had seen her mother struggle paying the bills months after months. Now Scott would help her and things could be much better.

Right after Natalie came back home, the phone ran and she answered, thinking it was Scott who forgot something. She froze when she heard the voice on the other end. She turned pale and screamed,

"Manuelito"

Then she inhaled so deep that she looked like she was going to faint. After a long pause she said very excitedly in Spanish,

"Yes, of course you can come! Tomorrow?

Manuel was one of Natalie's secrets that she never mentioned to Scott. He was her oldest son who stayed in Colombia with his father. He had dropped out of school when she left for the U.S. and went to live in a fishing town on the Caribbean coast with some friends. Now after roughing it for almost three years, he was coming to Miami on a student visa. Natalie was hardly aware of his plans until she got the call. He was now coming and Scott needed to know. Four children was a lot to swallow, five may very well destroy her wedding.

She immediately summoned Scott to tell him the news. She was crying when Scott arrived. He was so frightened with her unusual behavior that he felt relieved when she told him about her new son coming the next day. He simply said,

"I love you, and that's not going to change."

Natalie tried to downplay the situation by saying he was an independent young man who would quickly get a job and be on his own very soon. Scott did not give it any significance.

Natalie's excitement grew considerably with the arrival of her son. Manuel was barely 15 when she left Colombia, but when Natalie saw him at Miami International Airport she couldn't believe her eyes. He had grown into handsome young man; long blond hair, slim and serious. He was sad about living his country, but when he saw his mother so happy about his arrival and his little sister Maria turned into a vivacious young girl, he laughed and felt better. He was now a matured young man. Natalie waited until they got home to tell him about the wedding. She was afraid he would not come if he knew she was getting married. Much to her surprise, he was very understanding and accepted her marriage as something natural and positive.

Natalie and Scott's wedding was held at Scott's house exactly as it was planned. It was a small but beautiful ceremony. They turned their backyard and terrace into a colorful tropical garden with potted plants neatly arranged among the white round tables. They invited a small group of people; close friends like Teresa, Irma and her husband Jose, their daughter Nancy; and Natalie's good friend in her bad moments, Pedro. Scott invited his best friend Carlos Luna, who was going to be his best man. At six o'clock the minister arrive and the ceremony started.

Natalie looked stunning in her white satin dress adorned with laces. The dress was not long, but elegant and made her look younger and slender. Her hair was styled nicely with small white flowers looking like a crown. Her eyes were bright with happiness. Scott looked a little nervous but very elegant and handsome in a dark colored suit. Rosa and Maria, dressed in blue and pink, were the prettiest girls in the party. Adrian in his dark blue suit was looking at his mother lovingly with his dark pretty eyes. At six thirty the ceremony stared.

Natalie was a little nervous when the minister asked her:

"Do you, Natalie De La Cruz, take Scott Johnson to be your lawfully wedded husband to have and to hold, from this day forward, for better, for worse, for richer, for poorer, in sickness and health, until death do you apart?"

Natalie answered:

"Yes I do?"

And smiled at Scott with her adoring eyes, like she was dreaming. Then he asked Scott the same. He looked at Natalie with intense love and answered:

"Yes I do."

The minister then asked for the wedding rings. He then gave Natalie's ring to Scott, and asked Scott to repeat after him:

"With this ring I thee wed, and pledge thee my troth."

Then he gave Scott's ring to Natalie and she repeated the same thing. After the exchange of the rings he said:

"I now pronounce you man and wife. You may kiss the bride."

Scott put his arm around Natalie's waist, pulled her close to him, put his lips against hers and kissed her very passionately. She responded like wise. Everyone began to applaud while Scott and Natalie kissed for the first time as husband and wife. When they were finished, the minister said:

"I now I present you Mr. and Mrs. Johnson. May their love grow even more with each passing year."

It was a wonderful afternoon for all the family: One by one the girls, Eugenia, Rosa and Maria, hugged the newly wed. Adrian and Manuel followed, then the rest of their friends. Natalie cried a little when she saw her children so happy hugging Scott. Now life will be different and happy for Natalie. For the first time since she arrived in the United States she felt part of this country.

After the party, Scott and Natalie drove to West Palm Beach for their honeymoon. Irma would take care of the children during their absence. They were going to stay three days in a hotel on the beach. They arrived at midnight and Natalie couldn't see the ocean, but she could hear the waves when Scott opened the door of the balcony in front of the ocean. It was the most beautiful place in the world because she was with him.

"Do you like it sweetheart? You haven't said anything."

She put her head on his shoulder and answered,

"I am so happy, and I cannot find the words to describe how I feel. Everything is beautiful, like a dream because you are with me."

He kissed her on her lips, and they hugged with passion. The wind from the sea was blowing Natalie's soft brown hair. Scott told her that she was always beautiful no matter what. He opened a bottle of wine, went out to the balcony and sat next to each other on the chairs. They drank to their happiness. Suddenly, the moon came out from behind the dark clouds, illuminated the beach and painting a reflection over the ocean to infinity.

"Oh Scott, the moon is there, do you see how beautiful everything is around. Now we can see the waves."

Scott looked for a while at the miracle of nature that was making them feel closer to each other like never before.

"My dear let's go inside now, if you like."

"Yes, I would like to, but I have to change my clothes." She said smiling.

She entered the room, and went into the bathroom, while Scott smoked a cigarette still sitting on the balcony.

"My dear, where are you? Do you need help getting undressed?"

He asked laughing. She didn't answer, but she walked out slowly and a little timid, wearing a blue babydoll that captivated Scott.

"Oh Natalie, you are really beautiful,"

He said while he picked her up and laid her on the bed.

"Dear Natalie my wish is that we will be as happy for the rest of our lives as you are this night. I don't want you to ever look sad like you did sometimes in the factory."

"Don't talk about that please, now everything is different, we will be very happy, I am sure."

They kissed with intense passion. The wind outside was blowing against the glass window, but they didn't hear anything. Natalie bid farewell to her first wedding, to her desperate love for a man who made her life so miserable she had to leave her country. Now Natalie Johnson was in the arms of her "sweet love" Scott Johnson, the man who arrived one morning at that dark factory to rescue her. He freed her from suffering and brought her to a marvelous place close to the sea where love was still possible. That night their passion consumed their bodies and they lost all sense of reality. They came back to reality three days later when it was time go back to the world again.

CHAPTER 27

SCOTT'S CHILDREN

SCOTT'S HOUSE WAS VERY BIG and comfortable compared to Natalie's. It had three bedrooms upstairs and plenty of space on the first floor. Eugenia, Rosa and Maria took one of the bedrooms while Adrian was fascinated with his own room. Manuel, as Natalie had predicted, got a job and stayed in Natalie's little old house with a friend. The girls were very excited because their bedroom had a balcony overlooking the street. Like most teenagers, they loved to be able to keep an eye on what's going on outside. Natalie's bedroom was the prettiest she ever had.

One Saturday afternoon after they settled in, Natalie was waiting for Scott to show up with his two boys for dinner. Scott returned at 6 o'clock without the children. He kissed her without smiling. She noticed a strained expression in his eyes. They went to the living room and sat down on the sofa without talking. He looked very different from the happy man who left in the morning. She knew something was wrong, but she didn't question him; instead, she offered him coffee.

"Yes dear, thank you."

She brought the coffee with cream, no sugar, just the way he liked it. She came back and sat close to him, waiting for him to tell her what happened, but he was still silent. He was drinking his coffee. She caressed his hand. He looked at her with a little sad smile.

"Christine has taken the children," he said.

"It is not possible, she cannot do this." Natalie answered.

"But she did it anyway. I didn't find anybody in the house and a neighbor told me she had moved out, she didn't know where. She thinks they went to another city."

He finished drinking his coffee and started smoking a cigarette. He never smoked inside the house, but now he seemed very confused and anguished. He inhaled very deep on his cigarette. Natalie looked at him, she didn't say anything. She didn't know how to help him at this difficult moment. He stood up and walked away without looking at her, absorbed in his thoughts.

"I suspected I was going to have a problem," He said suddenly, "but I never imagined she would do that. She knows that I have custody of them, and it is a felony to do that."

"But why are they living with her?" He moved his head in disbelief. "I don't know, I was never supposed to trust her because she abandoned them when they were babies, but she swore she had changed. Besides I was working all the time and had little time for them. Now she has taken them, and I don't know what to do."

"You can talk with a lawyer and take her to court," Natalie suggested.

"Yes, but I don't know where she is. I think she could be in Virginia where her family lives, but I don't have the address."

"We can look for them, don't worry about it, everything is going to be okay."

"You don't understand," he said in a disappointed tone he never used with her.

She felt frustrated and didn't insist anymore. She left him alone while he continued smoking.

In the afternoon the girls set the table for a dinner that Natalie had prepared with great care. They noticed that Scott was walking alone in the yard. They asked their mother what happened to him. They all sat down to eat but Scott would not come.

"What happened mom," asked Rosa, "Is Scott upset at us?"

"No, don't think that. There is something very serious that troubles him."

"What is it mami?" Maria said "I don't like to see him like that."

"Me neither."

Natalie explained what happened to Scott's children.

"That's very sad," Rosa said, "but I think he can get them back, he is their father."

Adrian was listening and decided to go look for Scott. They both came back and Scott said,

"I guess this must be a special dinner if Adrian went looking for me."

And went to Natalie to give her a kiss. They all smiled and began to eat. During dinner, Scott asked about the children's school. After a long conversation, they decided the children would continue to attend the same school because they were in the middle of the school year, even though it was too far. At night when Natalie and Scott went to their bedroom, she was silent. Natalie couldn't find the right words to make him feel better. She felt that her English was poor and could complicate matters even more. She has to be extra careful when talking about serious issues with Scott. Early that afternoon, when she tried to console him, she said, "don't worry about it" but he may have interpreted it as "that's not important." Similarly, when Scott told Natalie, "You don't understand Natalie," she interpreted as "you don't understand enough English." There was a language barrier and Natalie was determined to break. By the time they went to sleep, they had figured out what each meant. He said, "I love you," she answered "te quiero."

CHAPTER 28

ANDRES HIDALGO

SCOTT AND NATALIE'S WEDDING WAS the biggest news in the factory in years. Not only was it unusual for a manager to marry a machine operator, it was even more strange for an American to tie the knot with an immigrant who spoke little English and had four dependent children. With the exception of a few ill-intentioned people, most workers in the factory were happy for them and congratulated them on their Cinderella story. Management, however, was not very pleased. A couple of weeks after the wedding, Scott was reassigned to the night shift, working from 10 pm to 7 am. This was a totally unexpected turn of events that would put considerable hardship on the newlywed.

It was definitely a punishment for Scott. His whole life was turned outside down; when he was working Natalie was sleeping and vise versa. Natalie continued working at the factory, but now she had to take the bus from their new house, which took her more than an hour each way. Scott decided he had enough and started to look for work elsewhere. Soon thereafter, he got a job offer in Orlando, Florida, some 5 hours from Miami by car. Natalie and the children were very excited with the possibility to move somewhere new and close to Disney World. After a long discussion the family decided it was best for everyone to move to Orlando. It was a sad and quiet farewell at the factory. Friends said goodbye one Friday afternoon and Natalie sobbed as she left the factory that ironically had given her some of the worst and best moments of her life in the U.S.

She never forgot the day she was suspended for writing poems to fight the dehumanizing effects of the perpetually running machines. But she also found among the turning pulleys of noisy machines the blue eyes of a great man who became her husband. A few days later, they loaded up a U-Haul trailer with some of their belongings, hitched it to his car, and drove up to Orlando. Scott was not very happy to leave his house behind so he put it up for sale. Manuel decided to stay in Miami living in the same house. Eugenia, by now an independent teenager, chose to stay in Miami sharing a small apartment with a female friend. She was working at a fast-food restaurant. Natalie was sad to leave Eugenia behind, but she knew it was probably better for the family since she didn't want to put too much pressure on Scott.

By the early 1980s Miami had become a beacon to people in Latin America and the Caribbean who were, for various reasons, dissatisfied with the social, economic and political conditions of their countries. In fact, Miami had become an enclave of Latin America, where Spanish was widely spoken. Orlando, on the other hand, had little influx from Latin America and therefore it was hard to get by without speaking fluent English. To Natalie, Orlando offered some challenges but she was determined to improve her English and get a better job.

The family rented a three-bedroom apartment on Aloma Avenue in Orlando and Scott started working immediately at a printing shop. Natalie was worried about her children's education. Up until now they have been attending the same Catholic school in Miami that did not ask a lot of questions about their immigration status. Now in Orlando they had to attend public school. To Scott, registering the children at school was a simple straightforward process. So the first chance he had, he took them to the local schools to register them. Adrian and Maria would be attending middle school, Rosa would be going to high school.

That day Scott came back at four o'clock to the apartment where Natalie was anxiously waiting. Adrian ran to her mother and proudly announced:

"We start on Monday, Mami. The bus will pick us up at the corner."

She didn't say anything when Adrian told her the good news; she just looked at the girls who walked in with serious faces. Scott kissed her saying:

"I am sorry my love that I didn't come to pick up you up, but I was caught up at work earlier. The schools only register new students until thee o'clock and I left earlier from work. He looked at her a little surprised; she seemed worried. He sat close to her and hugged her with affection.

"Why are you worried? Do you think we are going to have problems with the schools? Rosa told me that they still don't have a green card, but I thought they had student visas. Otherwise, they won't let them attend public schools. They have been here in the United States for a long time already."

"Yes, three plus years."

Natalie answered while looking at Rosa, who continued to stand next to Maria.

"Well that's good," Scott said, "Mrs. Smith, the lady that registered them, told me that they will call the children's school in Miami to transfer all the papers. This will take a few days, but in the meantime they can go to school. She was very nice, wasn't she Rosa?"

"Yes, she was nice."

Rosa said without smiling.

"You know Natalie," he said, changing the course of the conversation. "I have an appointment with a lawyer at five o'clock, to fix the problem I have with my children. I have to go immediately."

"Do you want to drink coffee or something Scott?"

"No, thank you, I don't have time because the rush hour traffic has started and his office is far from here. I will be back for dinner."

He kissed her and left in a hurry.

She was watching him as he was leaving. The girls were at her side while Adrian ran outside to roll skate

"Don't be late Adrian, remember, one hour only."

Okay mami, I will go only to the corner, I will come back soon."

Then she started talking to her daughters.

"What happened girls, why are you so silent?"

"You can imagine," Rosa said. "In that school I was so scared with that Mrs. Smith looking at us when she realized we were not Americans. I can't explain why she gave us permission to go to school. I noticed she did not believe us when we said we had student visas."

"Yes," Maria added. "I was so scared too, but finally she signed the application."

"Yes, but it was because of Scott, he is American, and she didn't dare rejecting us." Rosa said.

"But did you tell Scott that we are not residents yet?"

"Yes, I had to do it, because you didn't. I don't think that's good, you have to tell him the truth."

"Yes, but so many things happening at the same time; I didn't want to worry him even more with our problems, watching him so distressed for his children. When he solves his problem I will talk to him, and I am sure that he will understand my reasons."

"But which reason, mami? Why do you have to be silent about our situation in the U.S.?"

Natalie paused for a while, and Rosa understood that she was right.

"I don't know, I never thought that this problem would arise so fast."

"You knew mother, but you were probably afraid."

"Afraid of what?

"I don't know, but everything is going to be a problem now, I know that."

"Alright Rosa, come down, you too Maria. I have to make a decision about this problem. I will talk to him; I hope it is not too late. He knew I married him because I love him very much."

"I hope so mami," Rosa said, "Because that school will not be for much longer. When they find out that we don't have visas, they will call you mami, I know that."

"Please dear, don't be so distressed before this happens, I think everything will be okay. Let's don't talk about this anymore please."

The following week the children went to the new schools without any incidents. Rosa found an admirer whose name, Maria said, was Bill.

"Be careful Rosa, you are a pretty girl, but too young."

Natalie warned her.

"Mami, it is just a guy that looks at me, he probably wants to be my friend in school, that's all."

Natalie felt a better about her children being in school, and she was happy again in her new apartment. Scott went to Virginia for a couple of days to find out about his children. Natalie was hoping he could bring his children back soon. For the first time since she arrived in the U.S., she was staying home without working, which felt strange and unfair to Scott. He was now paying for everything. She did not want to become a burden for Scott and so she began looking for work. She was looking through the employment section of the local newspaper when she heard someone knocking at her door. She immediately opened the door thinking it was Scott with the children. She froze and turned pale in an instant. She then took one step back and tried to close the door, hesitated and finally spoke:

"What are you doing here, Andres?" She said in Spanish.

It was Andres Hidalgo, the man she had been in love with in Colombia and partly responsible for her being in the U.S. He smiled and looked at her as she regained her composure.

"I came to see you. You have changed a lot."

"Yes, I have changed a lot, and now I am married. Didn't you know that?"

"Yes, I knew it, your daughters told me before you married. I was at your other house in Miami and they wouldn't let me in. I don't understand why your daughters treated me like that."

"You were at my other house? They never told me." Natalie said.

They didn't want you to know about my visit. They thought that I would harm you."

Andres had an ironic smile on his face as he said that.

"Well they know how you were during your last visit. It was a painful memory for me, and for them also because they saw me suffer because of your attitude. Now you come back. What for?"

"I know, please excuse me; but we have to talk. Would you invite in?"

"Yes, come in but you cannot stay a for long. I don't know who gave you my new address."

Andres walked in and sat on the living room sofa. He looked around and then said:

"Beautiful apartment, congratulations! Irma gave me your address. I don't know why you are hiding from me. I know you are married and have the man you wanted. You have a good home, and I imagine he is a good husband who loves you, but that is not a reason to close the door on me."

"Well you don't have any reason to visit me, our time has passed you know that."

"It is true, I have made a lot of mistakes, but I just want you to know that I am sorry I was not able to be the man you deserve.

Natalie looked at him in disbelief.

"Listen Andres, I loved you before, and I left my country because of you. I wanted to finish with that relationship. I knew your temperament and we never could have been happy. Now everything has changed. The Natalie that you knew died the day you told me you felt bad when you were with me."

"Now I am happy, very happy, after many years of suffering and working alone for my children. You never loved me because you are very selfish to love anyone, only yourself. Leave me alone, please."

He was very serious while listening to her words, and told her in an angry tone that he knew Natalie didn't care about him anymore. He then added:

"I didn't make you suffer on purpose, it was the circumstances."

Suddenly, he changed his attitude and Andre's expression was that of a frustrated man.

"You know Natalie, I loved you very much, but this is the way I am. I know that you have every reason to be upset at me, but it is my destiny which I cannot change."

Natalie didn't answer, he was always a strange man, and she knew that he wasn't happy. Andres stood up to go. He didn't say anything else. He must have wondered how incredibly a woman could change her feelings. She used to love him a lot. Now she looked happy, pretty, and very indifferent toward him. Maybe he was supposed to leave the apartment and forget about being in her life ever. He extended his hand to say good-bye to Natalie. She did the same, and both looked at each other for the last time.

At this same moment the front door opened and Scott entered the house. He looked surprised to see the tall, dark featured man, with an arrogant presence, holding his wife's hand. Natalie pulled her hand away and went to greet Scott. He said hello to him and he gave Natalie a kiss on the cheek.

"Are you surprised dear?" Scott said. "You weren't expecting me today? You have a visitor, I am sorry to bother you, we will talk later."

Then Andres spoke with courtesy in perfect English:

"No, no, I have to go now, I came to say hello to Natalie and her children."

Natalie came back to reality and introduced them:

"Dear, this is Andres Hidalgo, a good friend from Colombia. Andres, this is my husband Scott Johnson."

They exchanged cordial greetings and shook hands.

Natalie looked at both men for a moment. Andres was tall, brown with and big dark eyes. Scott had blond hair and blue eyes, slender and strong body. They were facing each other. It was her past and present in a flash of time. The two men represented a bridge from the past to the future.

"Are you going to stay for a while in town?" Scott asked.

"No, I am leaving tomorrow. I stopped by to say hello and ask Natalie if she wanted to send anything to her family in Colombia."

Scott asked her,

"Sweetheart do you have something to send to your family?"

"No," she said, looking at Andres, "because I wasn't expecting you, I didn't buy anything. I would have liked to send something."

"It is okay, maybe on another occasion, next year possibly. Sometimes my company sends me here for conferences."

"Thank you for coming and making the offer."

Natalie said smiling.

Andres Hidalgo said goodbye to both, and Natalie accompanied him to the door.

"You have a good trip, and say hello to your family."

He walked away and disappeared in the parking lot—and from Natalie's life.

CHAPTER 29

CHILDREN WITHOUT SCHOOL

Scott was obviously not pleased with the scene he found when he opened the door. Natalie had a lot of explaining to do, but first she asked about his children.

"Yes, thanks God I got to see my children,"

Answered Scott.

"But why did she take the kids?"

"I don't know, she said because she didn't like her job in Miami. My lawyer is going to talk to her, and he said he could arrange something. I don't want to take her to court but if she doesn't cooperate, I will."

"How long do you have to wait?"

"I don't know, maybe a few weeks."

Then the inevitable question came:

"Listen Natalie, why was Andres holding your hand as though you belonged to him?"

"We were just saying goodbye. Andres belongs to the past. He is out of my life for good. You don't have worry about it, it all in the past.

"You never told me anything about your past, and I have the impression that you don't trust me. Why sweetheart?"

"You know I don't like to talk about the past. You know Scott, I love you very much, and perhaps one day when you are calmer I will tell you about my past. There wasn't anything special between us, only work, problems, and a few cheerful times; for this reason I didn't say anything, but if you want I will tell you."

Scott did not insist and preferred to leave the unpleasant conversation for later.

156

A few days went by, and one afternoon Maria came from school and broke the news to her mother:

"We were suspended from school. They found out the we don't have visas."

There was a mixture of anger and sadness in her voice.

"This cannot be," replied Natalie, "they would call me before they did that."

"They called us to the office today," Maria said, "to tell us that we need a certified paper, signed or something, I don't know. Mrs. Smith said that she was sorry but we cannot come back to school."

Rosa later came with the same story. Since they were unable to prove their legal status in the United States, the children were not allowed to go to school. The world was crumbling around Natalie. Just when she thought that things were going to get better, her children were sent home, denied of their right to a basic education. This was not what Natalie expected of the U.S. Leaving children without an education because their immigration status was simply unacceptable and cruel to Natalie. But Rosa understood it:

"We need the Green Card, or permission from Immigration. Mrs. Smith made that clear."

"But you have to go to school." Natalie said.

"No mami, the law is like that, we are not from this country."

There was anguish in her juvenile voice, and Natalie saw it in her eyes. Her daughter was suffering and she felt guilty. She had to fix this situation at any cost. Rosa noticed her mother's sadness and tried to console her. She hugged her and said lovingly:

"Don't you worry mami, I am sure that Scott will help you fix this problem."

"Do you think so? I thought that he might be disappointed with me for not telling him the truth about our status here, and probably he won't want to see me anymore. I don't know."

"He loves you a lot, and he will do everything for you."

When Scott came back home in the afternoon, Adrian opened the door and told him immediately:

"We can't go back to school."

"There must be a mistake; I will call the schools tomorrow first thing."

Later Natalie told him what he suspected:

"My children don't have the papers they need."

She finally admitted it, looking away to avoid his eyes. The following day Scott called the schools to find out and he got the same response. The children were sent home because they did nor have legal permit to stay in the U.S. Natalie was silent, waiting for Scott to reproach her for not telling him truth from the beginning. However, he calmly said:

"Tomorrow I'll go to Immigration office to get the application you need to apply for a green card, which you are entitled as the wife of an American Citizen. Don't you worry, everything is going to be fine."

"Are you doing this for me, Scott?"

Natalie asked looking at him with love.

"Yes, this and more, everything you need."

"Thank you, Scott."

"Remember Natalie what I said the night we married, I don't want to see you sad, smile please, you are my love."

Natalie smiled happy again, and both sat on the sofa. She hugged him and they kissed. A thunderstorm was raging outside but they were oblivious to everything except their love. Once again they felt their love will prevail and their lives together will be wonderful.

CHAPTER 30

DEPORTATION

TWO MONTHS WENT BY BEFORE the immigration papers were ready to be submitted. They had to go through what seemed to be a never-ending process. Natalie had to write to her country to get their birth certificates, which took more than two weeks. Then they went to the police station with the children to take their fingerprints. Pictures and medical exams were also necessary. Scott was getting tired, but he didn't say anything because he understood it was necessary so his wife and family would be able to stay in the U.S.

The children were very bored at home not being able to go to school and feeling like outcasts. They avoided other children in the neighborhood for fear of not knowing what to say when the inevitable question came: "So which school do you go to?" Maria was particularly affected; she spent many hours sitting in front of the TV. One day she said half jokingly:

"Mami I'm going to get old sitting here, watching TV all the time."

Adrian made some friends and played with them in the neighborhood, but he felt bad when they asked him about school. He didn't know what to answer, and when they insisted, he turned around and went back home. Rosa, who was always very interested in school, found out about a community education program nearby where they did not ask about immigration status. She immediately enrolled in a fast track high school program. She liked the place and made friends quickly. Soon she was on her way to earn her high school diploma this way and was taking prep courses to enter a community college.

Finally, the long-awaited day arrived. Everything was meticulously arranged in a file folder to be submitted to Immigration by Scott. The entire family was very excited and anxious that morning during breakfast. Scott made the announcement that everybody knew:

"Today I will go to Immigration to turn in the applications and request the authorization to get the children back to school."

Natalie looked at him a little nervous and asked if she could go with him.

"No, I think it is better if I go by myself. Later, if needed, I will take all of you with me."

Nobody said anything; they all looked at him, their eyes reflected hope. They were about to take the giant leap from an outcast family, living in the shadows of an alien society they did not understand, into the legal world they could explore at will without fear of being exploited, abused, arrested or deported to their country of origin. Natalie accompanied her husband to the door and hugging him said:

"I love you a lot, and I appreciate all of the effort you have made, helping my family and me with this problem."

"But it is nothing sweetheart, I only want this problem to be solved soon, because the children are worried and I don't like to see them like that."

"Yes, you are right, this is the most important thing, but just want to say thank you, with all my heart."

He kissed and hugged her, saying,

"Wish me good luck Natalie, this afternoon when I come back, I hope everything would be solved."

"Good luck, and don't forget to call me."

But Scott did not call. The day went by and the phone did not ring. Natalie tried to occupy her mind reading newspapers, especially the employment sections. Ever since she arrived in Orlando she has not ceased looking for work. She even got a few interviews at local supermarkets and stores but she had been turned down mainly because of her limited English. That day she remembered a Puerto Rican neighbor who mentioned to her she could get her a job as a maid at a large hotel near Disney World. At first she did not pay much attention, but now she decided to pay her a visit and find out about the job. It may not be too appealing, but it would bring in some badly needed money, she thought. The lady was very helpful and promised her she would find out that same week. Natalie came back to the apartment anxious to know about Scott but Maria answered,

"No mami, Scott didn't call. I hope everything was okay."

"God, I cannot loose everything I have now, it would be terrible. I couldn't take that."

It was five o'clock in the afternoon when Scott walked into the apartment. He didn't have to speak; everybody knew things went wrong. After saying hello to everybody and kissing Natalie, he called her into their bedroom and let out his frustration:

"Natalie, Immigration didn't accept the applications because you and your children are on the computer ready to be deported. Everything was too late, you waited too long to submit the papers. Now the only thing left for me to do is to go with you to your country. I will sell the house and we will leave before they deport you."

Natalie could not utter a word. Scott was clearly frustrated and nervous. He started to smoke a cigarette, turned the TV on and sat down to watch it.

"Don't you have anything to say, Natalie?" he asked.

"Yes, but you are not supposed to think of abandoning your country because of me. We can get a lawyer, they always find ways to fix the problems."

He stood up again, and he answered angrily,

"No, I don't want to do anything else. I have just spent a horrible day at the immigration office when those people refused to take your applications. I'll tell you something, I will not sign anymore papers."

He had an unusual stern expression in his eyes when he said those last words. Then he turned his back and left the room.

"Please Scott, listen."

Natalie tried to stop him, but he continued walking towards the front door. She heard the door shut and the sound of his car leaving the parking lot. Scott was leaving in frustration. He just couldn't take the pressure any longer. He was an American unfamiliar with the problems confronted by immigrants escaping intolerable situations in their countries or looking for a better future. Natalie went to her bedroom and shut the door.

Natalie sat close to the window, her favorite place. Her mind was now traveling fast, reaching into the most remote corners of her imagination. Her happiness was extinguished before her eyes. Tears ran down her pale face, and for a moment she felt like she did before she met Scott. She could lose him, no doubt. Suddenly, an idea came to her mind. She stopped crying, stood up, dashed across the room and reached for the telephone directory. In an instant Natalie the fighter took over—the one who arrived in the U.S. with $1300 and four children. She didn't know it or even suspected it, but beneath her soft and sweet character lay a tough woman with steel determination. Once again she felt full of courage and ready for battle.

She had come a long way to let this incident wreck her life. She browsed for a while through the yellow pages, not exactly knowing what to look for. Then a something caught her attention: "GUIDE AND HELP FOR LATIN PEOPLE IN THE USA." She called immediately, and a friendly voice answered in Spanish. Natalie explained everything without omitting any details about her case. The nice lady recommended a lawyer who knew a lot about immigration law and gave her his phone number. She didn't loose any time and called first thing the following morning. She got an appointment the same day. Scott had arrived late the previous night and was gone to work by the time Natalie got up. She called her children and told them to get ready for an important appointment they all needed to attend.

"We are going to see a lawyer to fix our immigration problem." She announced.

They all understood the seriousness of the matter and were ready in minutes. Natalie called a taxi and while they were waiting she took the file folder with all the papers that Scott had left on the coffee table. She also made sure she had the checkbook Scott had given to her to be used in an emergency. The taxi arrived and Natalie Johnson with her family departed toward the office of a lawyer who may help them get their lives back on track.

They arrived a few minutes early at Anthony Sanford Law Office. It was an elegant office with expensive-looking furniture. Natalie looked around and noticed that Mr. Sanford was a prestigious lawyer. She wondered if she had enough money to pay him. His secretary said hello and invited them into his office. Natalie was worried about making a good impression so the lawyer would take the case. She looked at her children and saw them so tensed that she had to sheer them up:

"Come on guys, put a smile on your faces, everything will be okay."

Mr. Sanford was about thirty-five years old, blond hair and blue eyes. He welcomed them with a friendly and impressive greeting:

"Sigan y siéntense por favor," perfect Spanish.

Natalie immediately realized she had won the first battle.

"Mrs. Johnson, remember that I am here to help you. Tell me about your case and I will see what I can do."

She smiled and her white teeth were more noticeable because of her red lips. For a moment Natalie was tense, she grabbed the edge of his desk with both hands, then she relaxed, placing them on her purse. She went into every detail from the moment she arrived to the U.S. until the applications were rejected by Immigration.

"But, are you married to an American Citizen?" The lawyer confirmed.

"Yes, but they said my children and I were going to be deported. They didn't accept the papers, my husband is very upset."

"Please, can you show me all the papers?"

She gave him the folder containing the papers. He started to review them very carefully, analyzing every page. He took a long time studying them, and for a while he seemed to forget about Natalie and her children. His silence made her tense again. The lawyer's face was serious but relaxed, without demonstrating any emotion. She, on the other hand, was going through one of the tensest moments of her life. This could mean the difference between a shameful deportation and full citizenship in the country they have chosen to live the rest of their lives. If Mr. Sanford said he couldn't do anything about it, she would have to go perhaps to another country with her children because she was not going to allow Scott to leave his country on her account. She didn't even have any money or a job now. Mr. Sanford finished examining the documents, and Rosa touched her mother's arm, bringing her back to reality.

Mr. Sanford smiled and said,

"I understand that you are worried. Immigration matters always take time, but do you want me to tell you something?"

"Please I am listening."

Her voice barely audible, she was waiting for the worst. She didn't even dare looking at her children, who were mute in anticipation. The man picked up all the papers, put them inside the folder, and stated his verdict parsimoniously:

"Mrs. Johnson, nobody can take you or your family away from this country!"

She was speechless. Such as straight answer was not what she was expecting to hear.

"Are you listening, mami?" Rosa said, "They can't deport us from this country."

The lawyer smiled looking at the girl.

"Yes, did you hear your daughter? This girl is very intelligent."

"Mr. Sanford this is a great news! The best. What do we have to do now?"

Natalie asked.

"Well you have to sign the applications, and your husband must come tomorrow to see me. My secretary is going to give him an appointment. I will charge you three hundred dollars for this. You can give me one hundred and fifty now. When you receive your appointment for immigration, you to pay the balance. Is this okay with you?"

"Oh yes, sure."

Natalie opened her purse, took out her checkbook and made a check payable to Anthony Sanford.

Suddenly, Maria intervened:

"When will we be able to go back to school?"

He looked surprised at Maria and asked:

"Do you mean you don't go to school now?"

"No, they suspended us two months ago."

The lawyer frowned and asked Natalie:

"Is it true that your children are not attending school now?"

"Yes, Mr. Sanford, it is true. They have been in the house for over two months."

"That's inconceivable! Don't you know that in this country children cannot be kept out of school? Nobody can deny your children the right to public education. Tell me the name of the school please, and I will call Tallahassee immediately, and rest assure they will be back in school tomorrow."

"Thank you, Mr. Sanford, you don't know how happy I am. The children have suffered long enough. I thought nobody could help us with this problem."

"About your husband, what did he say about this whole process?"

"Well, he helped us fill out the immigration papers, but now he is upset because they rejected the papers."

Then, he called her by her first name:

"Natalie, tell your husband that your problem will be solved soon. I will call and let you know."

"But he said that he won't sign anymore papers."

He laughed:

"I'm sure that once he hears the good news he will sign many papers. Do you think he wants to lose you?"

"I don't think so."

She smiled, answering the contagious smile of the layer who put her life back together in less than an hour. She then realized how valuable education and knowledge about this new country could be. She knew it was probably illegal to deprive children of their education in the country she admired so much. Natalie was happy again, leaving behind the nightmare of their children staying home without an education.

CHAPTER 31

GREEN CARD

NATALIE AND SCOTT QUICKLY FORGOT the immigration incident and were once again happy together. When Natalie told Scott about the lawyer and how easy he made it for them, he hugged her and said he would sign anything for her. The schools called them back saying they would excuse their absences. Rosa decided to continue in the same program since she was close to getting a high school diploma.

Bills were mounting and Natalie was desperate to find a job to help Scott with the expenses. After trying unsuccessfully to find a job close to her apartment, she decided to apply for the job her neighbor suggested—as a maid at the hotel near Disney World. She needed a temporary job to help Scott and this seemed like her only option. Her neighbor recommended her and she was hired after a short interview. She was asked if she was capable of cleaning eight rooms per day, and she said yes. "How hard can that be?" She thought.

She was given two days of training with an experienced maid, and the third day she found herself in a long and solitary hallway pushing a housekeeping cart full of all things necessary to make the hotel rooms look impeccable. She was expected to vacuum; change the sheets and do the beds; wash and disinfect the toilets, sinks and bathtubs; dust and clean everything in the room. The first day she was only able to do four rooms. By the end of the week, she was doing six. The second week she was trying harder but she was not able to do more than six. Other maids had to help her at the end of the day. She was trying her best, working nonstop to meet her quota, but to no avail. She was leaving her apartment at 5 a.m., sharing a ride to the hotel with her Puerto Rican neighbor, working all day and coming back at 6 pm exhausted. She was loosing weight and becoming increasingly tired. Into her third week, her supervisor, a voluminous lady with a nasty attitude, walked into the room she was cleaning and demanded the bathtub be washed again. Natalie replied that she had just cleaned it and it was spotless. She vociferously insisted and threatened to fire Natalie on the spot. Natalie looked into her eyes and said firmly without screaming:

"I came to this country to work and take care of my children but I am not a slave."

The last words must have shocked her for she turned around and left the room in silence. Natalie continued working in the hotel without meeting her quota for a couple of weeks more until her lawyer called them and suggested they go to Miami to summit their immigration papers.

"In Miami they would process these documents within two months and you can be a permanent legal resident of the United States in three months."

He told her. She took this opportunity to resign from her job she knew it was too physically demanding for her, and to convince the family to go back to Miami where she could get a better job. It was a hard decision, especially for Scott who was already comfortable with his job. The kids were not very happy with the idea either, particularly Rosa who by now had managed to get her high school diploma and was going to attend a community college. At the end of the day, however, they all understood that immigration matters took precedence over everything else. Soon they started making preparations to move back to Miami.

Two weeks later they were back in Miami, living in a three-bedroom apartment they rented close to her old house. They quickly took care of the immigration papers, which were accepted at the Miami branch of the Immigration and Naturalization Services, as suggested by the lawyer. After the papers were processed, they received a letter stating that Natalie and his children had a legal immigration status, which entitled them to work and study in the United States. In short, she was going to receive the long-awaited "green card" soon. There was a general state of celebration and jubilance in the Johnson / De la Cruz household. Natalie was simply overjoyed. She went out to walk the streets of downtown Miami and everything felt different. She was no longer afraid to visit banks, schools, government offices and potential employers. She was now Natalie

Johnson, married to a great American man, and free to apply for any job she wished.

Her first move as a legal immigrant was to apply for an office job at a temporary employment agency. At the same time she started taking English classes for Speakers of Other Languages at Miami Dade Community College. Soon she was working as a temporary office assistant during the day and studying English at night. Ironically, she was attending the Downtown Campus located right in front of the restaurant she used to work when she first arrived in Miami. She was a proud student now. She remembered how many times she watched the students coming and going—wishing she could do the same—while she served breakfast to old people for 25-cent tips, and put up with a cruel cook who made her life miserable.

Scott also found a job at large home-improvement store as an assistant manager. He had sold his house before they moved back to Miami and was waiting to settle down to start looking for another house. Rosa missed her school in Orlando but, according to Maria, in reality she was in love with Bill, the boy she met there. She began working at a fast-food restaurant. Maria was attending a public high school and working after school at a supermarket nearby. They were both helping out with the bills at home. Adrian was also attending public school and playing football as any other American boy. Natalie's family has been fortunate and she thanked God for that.

CHAPTER 32

THE CONCLUSION

SEVERAL YEARS LATER NATALIE AND Scott found themselves attending Adrian's graduation as an architect at the University of Miami. She wept and thanked God for all the wonderful things she had received in life. Her youngest son was graduating from an American university, something she only dreamed of while she toiled to pay the rent and put food on the table. This event marked Natalie's highest achievement in the U.S. His youngest and most vulnerable child turned into a studious and committed architect. Maria, the cheerful little girl with a contagious smile, started working as a receptionist at an insurance company and ended up running her own successful firm a few years later. Rosa, the smart girl who was always advising her mother, married Bill, moved there and graduated from college. Eugenia studied travel and tourism and led a successful travel career. Manuel, the high school dropout, surprised everybody by getting a bachelor and a master's degree at a prestigious university.

Natalie was now working full time at a cruise line company where she was doing what she loved the most: writing. She was in charge of answering written requests and complaints from customers, which she replied more poetically than necessary. She used her position to travel constantly on the company ships to many wonderful places around the world, always in the company of Scott. She also managed to write some books, three of which have been published, and the last one you have it in your hands. Scott made a career at the home-improvement store. His children continued to be raised by their mother in Virginia since he thought a legal battle would have been painful for everyone.

Natalie and her children were now citizens of the United States thanks to Scott and her perseverance throughout the years. Her love for her children and the promise of a new life made her to leave her country with four children and very little money. Almost miraculously she managed to succeed. Her life has had many ups and downs but one thing has remained constant: her love for her family and Scott.